RESTLESS

Mahogany Star

RESTLESS

Second Edition

ISBN: 978-0-9789599-3-7

Ebony Prose Press www.ebonyprosepress.com

For My Grandmothers, Lucille, LillyMae & Joyce

"Life imitates art far more than art imitates life"

— Oscar Wilde

Table of Contents

ACKNOWLEDGMENTS

I am thankful to God, who created the Heavens and Earth, for the ability to use my imagination and create stories that some find good enough to read and enjoy. I am also thankful for my better half, Mike; you are everything to me; I love you and the life we've created so much. My children, Michael-Jalen and Madison-Leigh, my heart and soul, I couldn't love you more if I tried. My mother, Maxina, my best friend, I love you so very much, and I'm so grateful for our life together. My sister, LaTeacha Monique, and my niece, Mikaylah, the extension to my little family unit. I love you both.

My cousin, Travis McCord, looking forward to the day you are free, I love you.

My Colon, Rozier, Porter & Martin family, your support means the world to me, and I love you.

My family, sister-friends who make my life sweeter with their presence: Bev, Sadri, Cassandra, Jill, Melena, Taisha R, Taisha M, Iasia, Keisha, Shantel, Connie, Kelly, Nagina, Luanda, Nailaja,

Twanna, Taywanna, Lorraine, Sasha (Sunjilise), Barbara, Kim, Kandece, Angelita, Bebe, my sister Shamecka & Teri, Dr. J Gil & Donnamarie, My Pastor's the Holmes, and my UTBAA church family.

To my grandmothers: The late Lucille L. (Mommy), you are my best friend, the light of my life, and the strongest woman I have ever known. I'm so grateful for you, your wisdom, guidance, protection, and prayers. I know my life is a result of your prayers. I love and miss you so much.

Grandma Mae, if the sun came from the sky and took human form, it would be you. You radiate warmth and love. You have been a staple of comfort and love in my life. You're everything good, and I love you.

Grandmother Joyce: I was born on your birthday, your first of many grandchildren. The older I get and the more I get to know you, the more I see myself. You write; you're creative. I'm thankful for our time, and for the ability to learn more about you. I love you.

PROLOGUE

The water was still warm when it stopped feeling like anything at all.

That's the thing nobody tells you about drowning. It doesn't announce itself. It settles over you quietly, like a heavy blanket, and by the time you understand what's happening, your body has already made its peace with it.

I was still in the tub. I could feel the porcelain curved against my spine, the water at my ears, and the particular stillness of a room where someone has already decided what's going to happen. My fingers wouldn't close. My legs wouldn't push. Something in the wine had done that — whatever he'd put in it, working through me now like concrete setting in my veins. I didn't know. I'd been dancing. I'd been celebrating. I'd poured glass after glass of what I thought was a farewell gift and I hadn't tasted anything wrong. That was the cruelest part, I'd been happy when it reached me.

Sebastian moved around the bathroom with the unhurried ease of a man completing a task he'd been planning for months. He folded a towel. Set it on the rack. Adjusted the edge so it hung perfectly even. That small, precise gesture said everything. He wasn't panicking. He wasn't grieving. He was tidying up.

He crouched beside the tub, and I watched his face come level with mine. Those eyes. I'd spent five years trying to find warmth behind them, and now I understood — there was nothing to find. The cold wasn't something he hid. It was the whole of him.

"You really shouldn't have gone looking." His voice was low, almost gentle. Therapeutic. The same register he used when he told me I was overreacting, that I was too sensitive, that I needed to rest. "The silver drive, Eve. That was a mistake."

I wanted to speak. The word please was somewhere at the back of my throat, small and useless.

He tilted his head, watching me the way he watched quarterly reports — looking for where the numbers stopped adding up. "I want you to know that I do respect your instincts. Professionally." He paused. "You just applied them at the wrong time."

The water was in my ears. That's what I remember most clearly, not the cold, not the weight, but the sound it made. Everything above the surface had gone muffled and distant, like the world was happening in another room. My own heartbeat was the loudest thing left.

The ceiling above him was white. I focused on it. A single water stain in the far corner shaped like nothing in particular. I thought about Grandma Locust's kitchen ceiling, the one with the hairline crack she'd been meaning to fix for a decade, the one I'd stared at from the floor as a child when the world was too loud and that kitchen was the only quiet place I knew.

Sebastian stood. He smoothed the front of his shirt the way he always did — one flat palm, downward, deliberate. Then he leaned over me one last time, and his lips touched my forehead. Dry.

Weightless. The kind of kiss you give a photograph.

"Goodbye, Eve."

He said it like he was leaving for the airport. Like there was a car waiting downstairs and he had a meeting in the morning, and this was simply the end of an evening. He walked out of my line of sight, and then I heard his footsteps cross the marble floor, and then I heard nothing.

The water moved in a slow circle near the drain.

I've tried to explain what happened next to Dr. Chen, and every time I do, I run out of language for it. You drift. That's the closest I can get. You leave the weight of your body behind like a coat dropped in a doorway, and then you're somewhere above it all, looking down. I could see the tub. I could see myself in it — hair fanned out, one arm draped over the porcelain edge, the other hand found my fingers grazing the tubs floor. I think I looked peaceful in a way I hadn't looked in years.

There were voices. Not voices exactly — more like a current running beneath everything, something pulling my attention the way a sound in another room pulls you out of sleep. Watch. Stay with it.

Watch what your life was.

I watched.

I watched the bathroom tile, the folded towel, the wine glass on the vanity with its dark red ring. I watched the version of me lying still in the water. And somewhere in the watching, something in me refused it. Not loudly. Not with any drama. Just a quiet refusal, like a door that won't quite close all the way no matter how many times you push it.

I don't know how long I was there.

I know Kiki found me. I know there was noise after that — her voice breaking in a register I'd never heard from her before, her hands on my face, cold tile against my cheek. I know there was an ambulance. I know I was somewhere between leaving and staying, and she pulled me back across that line with nothing but her own sheer refusal to let me go.

But that comes later.

What I want you to understand first, before Kiki, before the hospital lights, before any of it — is the moment Sebastian kissed my forehead and walked away. The ease of it. The tidiness. The way a man can love you into a life and then fold you up like a shirt and smooth every crease until there's no evidence you were ever there at all.

That's where this story lives. In that bathroom. In that water. In that dry, weightless goodbye.

Everything else is how I got there.

Chapter 1

THE PERFORMANCE OF NORMAL

Several months before Sebastian said goodbye, I was sitting in a restaurant on the Upper West Side with my third glass of Chardonnay sweating rings into the white linen tablecloth, and my cousin Kidada affectionately known as Kiki was talking. She was always talking. That was the thing about Kiki, silence made her nervous, so she filled it the way other people filled closets, with everything she couldn't bring herself to examine too closely.

"Okay, but did you see what Gabrielle wore to the BET pre-show?" Kiki leaned forward, diamonds flashing on her wrist. "Because I need someone to explain who approved of that look, because it wasn't a stylist, it was a grudge. They had her looking downright stupid."

I laughed. Or I made the shape of a laugh, the sound, the tilt of my head. I was getting good at that shit.

The restaurant hummed around us, with low lighting, jazz underneath the conversation. I circled the stem of my wine glass with two fingers and let Kiki carry the evening while I sat inside my own silence and called it dinner.

The thing about having secrets is that they don't stay still. They move around in you. They find the tender spots. I had three of them working on me that night: Cam, the Valium I'd taken before I left the apartment, and the funny way Sebastian had looked at me that morning across the kitchen island, like I was an item on a list he hadn't decided whether to keep. He'd looked away before I could hold his gaze. At the time I'd called it distraction. Looking back now, I understand it for what it was — a man who had already made up his mind and was simply waiting for the right moment to act on it.

"Eve." Kiki snapped her fingers once, lightly. "You with me?"

"I'm here." I picked up my glass. "Keep going. The dress."

She gave me a look, that sharp sideways thing she'd been doing since we were twelve, but she let it go and kept going. She always lets it go eventually. That was her grace, even when she didn't know she was offering it.

She moved on to Lance's colleague's wife who had apparently shown up to a charity gala in a look that required a full ten-minute breakdown, and I nodded in the right places and refilled my glass when the bottle came back around, and underneath all of it I was drowning. Not in water. Not yet. In the coldness of a life that had stopped fitting me somewhere along the way and that I had kept wearing anyway, kept buttoning up each morning, kept presenting to the world with a straight hem and good shoes.

I looked at Kiki, her caramel skin catching the warm light, her laugh coming easy, her whole body leaning into the story she was telling — and I felt something hollow open up behind my ribs. She didn't know. Nobody knew. That was the bargain I'd made with myself: keep it contained, keep it clean, keep Sebastian's cruelty behind closed doors where it couldn't touch anyone else.

The Chardonnay was doing its job. The Valium would once again do its job later, when it was time to go home to Sebastian. Between the two of them, I could almost feel like a woman at dinner with her cousin, laughing about a bad gown, instead of what I actually was.

A woman already disappearing. Just too medicated to notice the cold closing in.

There was a Tuesday — not that Tuesday, a different one, three weeks earlier — when I'd been standing in the cereal aisle at the Whole Foods in Edgewater. I'd gone in for one thing. Walked out with nothing I really wanted or needed. Because somewhere between the organic granola and the Cream of Wheat, I'd just... stopped. I stood there with the cart handle in both hands and stared at the boxes and felt absolutely nothing, and then I felt everything, and then I started crying. Right there. Silently, the way Black women learn to cry in public — no sound, face almost still, just the tears doing what they needed to do while the rest of me kept it together. A woman with a toddler on her hip gave me a long, knowing look and kept moving. She didn't say anything. She didn't need to. We both knew what it was.

I stood there for another two minutes. Then I wiped my face with the back of my hand, straightened my posture, and pushed the cart toward the registers. I bought a box of Cream of Wheat I wouldn't eat, went home, put it in the cabinet, and never mentioned it to anyone.

That was the thing nobody saw. The Tuesday-afternoon version of me. The grocery store version. The one who sat in parking lots for ten minutes before going inside anywhere because she needed a moment to become the woman everyone expected to walk through the door.

Chapter 2

WHAT WE PRETEND NOT TO SEE

A few weeks later.

Candy. Apple. Red. Her lips were perfect. Too perfect. The candy apple red on Kidada's mouth was flawless, unmoving—as if nothing in her life dared to crack. Mine never looked like that. By the end of any night, my lipstick was always worn down, blurred at the edges... like evidence of something reckless.

As usual Kiki had been talking for forty minutes straight.

I know because I'd checked my phone twice under the table, angling the screen toward my lap like a teenager in class. The restaurant was loud enough to cover it — a warm, candlelit Italian place in the West Village that she'd chosen because the sommelier knew her by name. She liked that. Kiki liked all the things that confirmed the cozy suburban New Jersey life she'd built.

"So, Mila's publicist actually had the nerve to call mine," she was saying, breaking a piece of focaccia with her manicured fingers, diamonds flashing in the low light.

"Mine. As if I'm just supposed to absorb that kind of energy without a response."

"Mm." I lifted my wine glass and let the Chardonnay sit on my tongue for a second before swallowing.

She looked at me. "You're not listening."

"I am sis. Mila's publicist, the nerve."

She pointed the focaccia at me. "What's going on with you tonight?"

"Work stress." I said it too fast, the way you reach for a word you've already rehearsed. "Quarterly review coming up. I'm just in my head."

Kiki softened the way she always did when she thought she understood something. She set down the bread and folded her hands on the table, switching registers from gossip to concern like flipping a channel. "Eve. You work too hard. You know what you need?"

I already knew what was coming.

"A baby," she said.

There it was.

"Kiki—"

"I'm serious. You and Sebastian have been married for five years. You're in your thirties. Lance and I waited too long with Ethan, and I regret every month we wasted." She reached across the table and covered my hand with hers. "A baby changes everything. Gives you something to focus on that actually matters."

I looked at her hand on mine. The warmth of it. The good intentions. And underneath all of it, the specific exhaustion of being known by someone who didn't know you at all anymore.

"I'll think about it," I said.

She beamed. "That's all I ask."

I excused myself to the restroom ten minutes later and stood at the sink with the water running, looking at myself in the mirror. The restaurant noise was muffled back here — just a low buzz, like the city breathing through the walls. My reflection looked composed. Pressed silk blouse, low bun, dark eyes that held their shape even when everything behind them was pulling apart.

I thought about Cam.

I'd been thinking about Cam since forever, even more so when he'd sent me a single text. You good? Two words and I'd carried them around for three days like they were something I'd found and didn't know where to put them down.

I dried my hands, went back to the table, and told Kiki I wasn't feeling well.

"The quarterly work thing. My head is splitting. I think I just need to go home and sleep." I was already reaching for my bag.

She looked at me with that expression she had, the one caught between buying it and knowing better. Then she squeezed my arm and told me to take care of myself and text her when I got in. I kissed her cheek and walked out into the night air, and the lie sat so lightly in my chest that I barely felt it anymore.

I didn't go home.

I stood on the sidewalk outside the restaurant and pulled out my phone. Three days I'd been carrying his two words around. Three days of putting the phone down, picking it up, talking myself out of it. I was tired of talking myself out of things, especially things that felt good like Cam.

I typed: I'm good. Are you around tonight?

His response came before I'd even made it to the corner.

Cam: Yeah. Waiting on you.

Me: Lies.

Cam: Come through Eve. You know I got you.

Three words, *come through Eve*. That was so him, no extra layers, no strings attached. Simply: come through. As if it were nothing. As if it were easy. As if I hadn't spent the last five years married.

Like no time had passed at all, and just like it hadn't, I got in a cab heading to Brooklyn before I could change my mind.

The taxi crossed the bridge, and I watched Manhattan shrink in the rear window, the lights pulling away like something receding. Washington and Lafayette, Brooklyn came up slow and familiar, the shift in the air, the different rhythm of the streets, the way the buildings that used to be low stretched to new buildings that were taller and the sky got wider. I gave the driver the address from memory, though I'd never had to work to remember it. Some things just live in you like that.

Cam buzzed me up without asking who it was. He already knew.

His apartment was on the third floor of a converted brownstone on a quiet block, and it smelled the way it always did, cedar and something faintly mechanical, traces of whatever his day had been. He opened the door in a white tee and grey sweats, barefoot, and just looked at me for a second with that crooked smile doing its quiet work.

"You ate?" he said.

"Barely."

He stepped back to let me in.

There was a game on low in the background. A half-empty glass of water on the coffee table. His work boots by the door, still carrying some dust from whatever job site he'd been on. The whole space had the kind of lived-in ease that my Fort Lee apartment, with its clean lines and Sebastian's compulsive symmetry, had never once managed.

I felt something loosen in my chest just standing in it.

He came to me in the kitchen doorway. No preamble, with the look that had melted me since we were teenagers. He just put his hands on either side of my face and looked at me the way he always did, like he was checking that I was actually there. Like my presence was a thing worth confirming.

"You, okay?" he asked.

"I will be," I said.

He kissed me, and the city noise went somewhere else entirely.

An hour later I was lying on my back, satisfied from his touch, his tongue and his stroke, staring at the ceiling, one arm folded behind my head, listening to the street sounds filter through the window he'd cracked open. Cam was beside me, one hand resting warm and heavy on my stomach, his breathing steady and slow. The room was dark except for the orange bleed of a streetlight through the curtains.

A year. We'd been doing this for a year, and I still hadn't figured out what to call it. The word affair felt too clinical, too soap-opera. The word love felt too true to say out loud. So, I didn't call it anything. I just kept coming back whenever I could make time.

We'd been everything to each other once. Since ninth grade, walking home from Boys and Girls High, hands locked until we hit my stoop where he always let go because Grandma Locust watched from the parlor window and he wasn't trying to lose his welcome. He was the first person outside of that brownstone who made me feel like I was worth paying attention to. Not performing for. Just being me.

Then I left. College upstate, then finance, then a version of myself I'd been building so deliberately that there wasn't room in it for a boy from Bed-Stuy who didn't have a plan yet. I told myself I was being practical. I told myself he'd understand. What I didn't say out loud — what I barely let myself think — was that I was ashamed of wanting something different from where I came from, and he was standing right in the middle of where I came from. So, I packaged him up with everything else I was leaving behind and kept moving.

What I found out later — through Grandma, through Bella, through the neighborhood telegraph that never stops broadcasting — was that the year after I left, Cam caught a charge. Minor narcotics distribution, a stupid decision in a stupid moment, the kind of thing that happens when a young Black man in Bed-Stuy loses his footing and nobody catches him in time. He did eighteen months. While I was pledging at parties and learning bond markets, he was learning what a cell sounds like at three in the morning. I carried that guilt like a stone in my shoe for years. I never called. I told myself it was because there was nothing I could do. The truth was I didn't want to look at what leaving had cost him.

When he got out, he built something. HVAC certification, then a license, then a reputation in the trades that people actually respected. He didn't come out bitter. He emerged focused. Purposeful. That was always Cam's way. Whatever life dealt him, he took it in stride and simply got back up without melodrama.

The first time I saw him again was three years into my marriage. A Bed-Stuy dive bar I'd wandered into after a dinner with a colleague nearby, the kind of place that still had a Budweiser sign in the window and vinyl booths that remembered the eighties. The air was thick with stale hops and damp wool. I was nursing a neat bourbon, my wedding ring catching the dim neon light, feeling like a beacon of everything I was supposed to be and everything I was quietly suffocating under.

When the bell chimed above the door, I looked up and we locked eyes, smiles spreading across both of our faces. Cam slid into the booth across from me like no time had passed and all the time had passed at once. He didn't look like the boy who'd walked me down Stuyvesant Avenue so many days after school. He looked like a man who had seen and been through things and decided to keep going anyway. He didn't say hello. He just looked at the ring on my finger, then up at my eyes.

"You look like you belong in a museum, Eve," he said, his voice low and unhurried. "Not in a place where the floor sticks to your shoes."

"Maybe I'm tired of museums," I said.

He reached across the table, his thumb grazing the back of my hand, just a fraction of an inch from the cold diamond. The heat of his skin was a shock.

"You should get up and walk out that door right now," he

said. But his eyes were a challenge I wasn't equipped to refuse.

"I know," I said. And I leaned forward anyway, the sticky wood biting into my elbows.

When he finally pulled me toward him, the first kiss tasted like salt and fifteen years of something that had never properly closed. I can't explain what happened to the vow in that moment except to say it didn't slowly erode —that shit shattered all at once, quietly, and for the first time in longer than I could account for, I felt like I could actually breathe.

On the first night we spent together afterward, Cam had been clear about one thing: he wasn't trying to break up my marriage. Those were his exact words, said without an apology. "I'm not your exit strategy, Eve. I just want to be with you when I'm with you.

That's all I'm asking for."

What started as something I'd convinced myself was purely physical had, over the course of a year, become the most honest relationship in my life. Cam, unpolished and unbothered by the things Sebastian used to impress people, brought a kind of vitality back into my days that I hadn't realized had gone missing. He wasn't a gap-filler. He was a reminder of something I'd left behind and never stopped wanting.

"You're thinking," he said without opening his eyes.

"I'm always thinking."

"Louder than usual tonight."

I turned my head to look at him. His profile in the dim light — the strong jaw, the low waves, the single dimple I couldn't see from this angle but knew was there. He looked peaceful in a way that cost him something to maintain around me, and I understood that now in a way I hadn't at the beginning.

"Kiki told me I should have a baby," I said.

He was quiet for a moment. "With Sebastian? That nig- that dude don't even want kids." He corrected himself and repeated what I had told him about Sebastian not wanting a family before.

It wasn't a question, but I answered it anyway. "She doesn't know about you."

"I know she doesn't." He opened his eyes and looked at the ceiling.

"You ever think about telling her?"

"And say what?"

He didn't answer that. He moved his hand from my stomach and laced his fingers through mine instead, and we stayed like that for a little while. I knew I had to leave. I'd known it from the moment I walked in. But I let myself have a few more minutes of this — the weight of his hand, the quiet, the room that felt like the only honest square footage in my entire life.

I got dressed while he watched from the bed, neither of us pretending this was something other than what it was.

"Be careful," he said when I was at the door.

"Always am."

He looked at me with something steady and unreadable. "You know

I mean that differently than you do."

I did know. I just didn't have an answer for it, so I let myself out.

The taxi back to Fort Lee felt longer than the ride over. I sat with my bag in my lap and my reflection ghosted in the window and thought about what careful meant when you were living two lives with equal fluency. The Valium was in a small orange bottle in the inside zipper pocket of my bag. I shook one out at a red light and swallowed it dry, the familiar bitterness dissolving at the back of my throat before the cab even crossed the bridge.

By the time I slid my key into the apartment door, the edges had gone soft. The medication didn't make me happy — it just made the distance between me and everything else manageable. Like watching your own life through slightly tinted glass.

Sebastian was in the living room. He was still dressed — charcoal trousers, dress shirt open at the collar — and he was standing by the window with a glass of something amber, looking out at the river. He turned when he heard me come in.

"You're late," he said. Not accusatory, it just sounded like an observation. Sebastian had a way of stating facts that made them feel like verdicts.

"Dinner ran long." I set my bag down by the console table and slipped off my heels. "Kiki talks."

He watched me cross the room. That calculating focus, the stillness in him that I'd once mistaken for depth. He set down his glass.

"Come here," he said.

I recognized the register of his voice. It had a particular quality on nights like this — smooth and low, stripped of any warmth. I recognized it the way you recognize weather before it breaks.

The bedroom was already arranged. That was always the word that came to me — arranged, like a room before a showing.

He was precise about these things, deliberate in a way that had nothing to do with me and everything to do with the theater of his own desire. The harness hung from the back of the closet door. The whip — a short-handled thing he'd ordered from some specialty catalog and presented to me once like it was a gift I should be grateful for — was on the dresser.

I stood in the doorway and let the Valium do what it could.

"You know what I want," he said behind me.

I did. I always did. That was the part that hollowed me out — not that he asked, but that I had learned to anticipate it so well I could have drawn a diagram.

"I need to shower." I almost pleaded.

"Make it quick, I've been waiting long enough for you to get home." He stated dryly.

I went through the motions the way I'd learned to, with the same professional competence I brought to everything in my life that required me to perform rather than feel.

At some point I caught my reflection in the full-length mirror on the wall opposite the bed. I don't know what made me look — some involuntary pull, the body checking in on itself. The woman looking back at me was composed, smooth-faced, holding her expression like a mask that had been on so long it had started to adhere. Behind her, Sebastian moved with his usual precision, conducting his invisible orchestra. The room smelled like his cologne and something colder underneath it.

The woman in the mirror didn't look afraid. She didn't look angry. She looked like someone waiting for a train — present in body, entirely somewhere else in every way that mattered.

I wondered when I'd learned to do that. I wondered if it was something I'd always known, or if he had taught me. It wasn't the same woman who was just in Cam's bed a few hours ago. That woman smiled and relished in the pleasure as Cam explored her body and provided her with so much bliss.

Afterward he was asleep within minutes, the way he always was, immediate and total, like a machine powering down. I lay beside him with my eyes open, the ceiling above me pale and blank, the only sound the faint sounds of horns from traffic going to and from across the George Washington Bridge.

I thought about Cam's apartment. The cedar smell. His hand on my stomach. Be careful.

I thought about how I must look.

I thought about how a person could be standing inside their own life and feel like a stranger looking in through the glass.

Then I closed my eyes and waited for the Valium to take the rest of it away.

Chapter 3

THE INNER CIRCLE

After texting my connect about picking up enough Valium to last the next week or two, I spent the afternoon with the two people who actually knew me: Justin and Isabella.

Justin found the table before I did, already settled into the corner booth at the Harlem spot he'd picked, a low-lit brunch place on 125th where the mimosas came in carafes and the staff knew better than to rush you. He was in a pink velvet blazer that had no business looking that good on a Sunday morning, and he was already halfway through his first drink when I slid in across from him.

"My bitch has arrived," he said, spreading his arms like I'd walked into his living room.

"You're already drinking," I said.

"It's brunch. Drinking is the point." He flagged down the waiter with two fingers. "Bella's parking. She texted from the garage. You know how she gets with parallel."

I settled in and pulled off my jacket, draping it over the back of the booth. The restaurant was warm and easy, the kind of place that didn't ask anything of you, just let you sit inside its noise and breathe. I hadn't realized how much I needed that until I was already in it.

Bella arrived twelve minutes later, slightly windswept, dropping into the booth beside Justin and immediately reaching for the carafe. She was a curvy Puerto Rican woman, one my oldest friends, we grew up together.

With long wavy jet-black hair, a small mole by her lip and silver hoops that caught the light, she had a way of walking into a room like she'd already owned and assessed it from the doorway.

"Traffic on the FDR was bananas," she announced. "I need to eat something before I can be a person."

Justin pushed the breadbasket toward her. "There fish. Be a person."

We ordered. The conversation moved the way it always did with the three of us, fast and overlapping, bouncing between Justin's ongoing war with his firm's management and Bella's latest client disaster, until Bella set down her fork and looked at me with that direct, unhurried attention she reserved for things that actually mattered.

"Okay," she said. "What's going on with you?"

I turned my mimosa glass in my fingers. The question wasn't aggressive; it never was with Bella. It just landed where it was aimed.

"I saw Cam," I said.

Justin was still for exactly half a second. Then he reached for his drink. "How was that?"

"It was — " I stopped. There wasn't a clean answer for it. "It was what it always is."

"Which means you went to Brooklyn," Bella said.

"Yes."

"And Sebastian thinks you were where?"

"Out to dinner with Kiki, which I was initially. He was home waiting with his usual demands when I got back. I had to pull a twofer since I had been with Cam." I kept my voice even. "We all know he tries to track my nights and my days."

Bella fascinated that. Justin made a sound that wasn't quite a laugh — more like a note he was filing away for later.

"Eve," Bella said, and her tone had shifted just slightly, the way a room shifts when someone opens a window. "I've been wanting to say something for a while now, and I don't want you to deflect or take it the wrong way."

"Then say it, Sis."

"Something is off with Sebastian." She said it plainly, without drama. "I know you know that. I know you've known it longer than you've admitted to yourself. But I'm saying it out loud because I think you need someone to say it out loud."

The table was quiet for a few seconds.

"Off how?" I asked, even though I already understood exactly what she meant.

"The way he looks at you at dinner. The way he talks over you in front of people and then smiles like he didn't. The way you check his expression before you say anything about your own plans." She kept her eyes on me. "That's not a man who loves you, Eve. That's a man who monitors you."

I looked at the breadbasket. The observation was accurate enough to sting in that specific way, not because it was new information, but because hearing it outside my own head made it real in a different register entirely.

Justin reached over and covered my hand with his. "She's not wrong."

"I know she's not," I said quietly.

"So, what are you going to do?" Bella asked.

That was the question, wasn't it? I turned it over and didn't answer it, and the three of us let it sit there on the table between the breadbasket and the mimosa carafe while the restaurant noise moved around us. I ate some of my eggs. Justin changed the subject to Marcus and their upcoming trip to Lisbon, and the conversation found its easier rhythm again, but the question stayed with me like something I'd slipped into my coat pocket.

Bella caught me in the restroom before I could get my coat. She leaned against the sink with her arms folded, watching me in the mirror the way she had since we were fourteen — like she already knew everything and was just waiting for me to stop pretending she didn't.

"You good?" she asked. Which, with Bella, meant I know you're not, but I'm giving you the chance to be real before I call you on it.

"I'm fine." I ran water over my hands.

She made a sound. "Eve."

I turned off the tap. Stood there a second. "I don't know what I am," I admitted, and it came out small in a way I hadn't planned. "I wake up every day, and I put on the face, and I attend team meetings for work, and I smile at the right moments, and I come home from being out and I do it all over again, and I genuinely do not know what's underneath any of it anymore. Like, if you stripped all of that away, I don't know what's left."

Bella didn't rush to fill the silence. That was the thing about her — she let things breathe. She just looked at me, steadily, and when she spoke it was quiet and exact.

"You're left," she said. "That's what's left. The real you, the one that existed before him, before the Valium, before you decided you had to be bulletproof to survive your own life. She's still there. She's just been quiet for a while."

She pushed off the sink and put both hands on my shoulders. "I need you to stop mourning the woman you are in that marriage, okay? That woman is suffocating. You are not her. You are so much more than that whole shitty ass situation."

My eyes burned. I blinked it back on instinct.

"You're allowed to cry in front of me, you know," Bella said, reading it exactly. "I've seen your ugly cry, bitch. You know I have.

It's not a thing."

A laugh came out of me before I could stop it. She smiled. That was Bella, she could pull a laugh out of you in the middle of the hardest moment and make it feel like grace instead of interruption.

"I don't know how to need people," I said. "I never learned how to do that without it costing me something."

"I know." She squeezed my shoulders and let go. "That's why you have me. Because I'm not going anywhere, and I'm not keeping score, and I'm not going to use what you give me against you." She picked up her bag from the counter and gave me one last look. “When you’re ready to actually talk — not around it but actually talk — call me. Day or night. I’ll be there.”

She walked out. I stood in front of that mirror for another minute, looking at myself. At the silk blouse and the careful makeup and the earrings I’d chosen because Sebastian liked them. I thought about what Bella had said: the real you is still there.

I wanted to believe her. I wasn’t there yet. But for the first time in a long time, I wanted to be.

I drove back to Fort Lee in the late afternoon, the GWB crossing slow with Sunday traffic, the Hudson wide and silver below. The brunch warmth was already wearing off by the time I pulled into the parking garage. I rode the elevator up with my jacket over my arm and my mind was still working on the edges of what Bella had said.

Sebastian was in the kitchen when I came through the door. Not cooking, he was just standing at the counter with his phone, dressed like he'd been somewhere, though he hadn't mentioned plans. He looked up when he heard me and something rearranged itself in his expression, quick and practiced.

"Hey," he said.

"Hey." I set my bag down on the console. "I didn't know you were going out."

"I had some things to handle." He turned back to his phone. "How was brunch?"

"Good. Justin sends his love."

"Mm." He was already elsewhere, attention back on the screen, and I would have thought nothing of it if he hadn't laughed, a low, private laugh, the kind you don't perform for a room. The kind that has an audience of one on the other end of a line. He caught it and cleared his throat and set the phone face-down on the counter.

I watched him do that. The deliberate placement. The small recalibration in his posture.

“Who’re you texting?” I asked, easy and light, like I was just making conversation.

"Josh from accounting." He opened the refrigerator and studied its contents like the question had already resolved itself. "He's got some questions about the quarterly projections. I told him I'd look at the numbers tonight."

"On a Sunday?"

"Numbers don't take weekends, Eve." He pulled out a bottle of sparkling water and turned, finally, to look at me. The expression was neutral, easy, completely assembled. "You eat enough at this brunch?" "I'm fine."

"You look tired." He said it the way he always did, not with warmth, but with that clinical observation that passed for concern.

"Get some rest tonight. You have a full week."

He picked up his phone from the counter and moved toward the hallway, and I stood in the kitchen and listened to his footsteps until they reached the bedroom and the door clicked softly shut.

I stood there for a moment. The kitchen was quiet and clean and perfectly arranged — his doing, always his doing, every container facing the same direction, every surface clear. I thought about the laugh. The way it had sounded genuine in a way his laughs around me almost never did. I thought about the phone going face-down before I'd even finished crossing the room.

Maybe. Sure. People texted their colleagues on Sundays. People laughed at things their colleagues said. I ran through the logic the way I ran through balance sheets, checking the columns, looking for where the numbers stopped adding up.

They stopped adding up at the laugh. Men should know that we women are way better at knowing and watching their moves than they are ours. We know their patterns, even when they change slightly and that laugh was out of character.

I went to the window and looked out at the river, the lights of Manhattan already coming on in the early dark. Bella's voice was still sitting in my chest. That's a man who monitors you. And I had spent five years monitoring him back, quietly, without naming it, the way you track a weather system you've learned to read. The pressure drops.

The air changes. You know what's coming before it arrives.

Sebastian had been watching me since the day we met. I had simply decided, standing in that kitchen with the sparkling water still condensing on the counter where he'd left it, that it was time to return the favor. Deliberately this time. With my eyes fully open.

I turned away from the window and went to pour myself a glass of water. The apartment hummed around me, clean and still and full of things I was only beginning to look at sideways.

Chapter 4

THE GILDED CAGE

Sebastian was on the floor beside the bed, watching me. That heavy, unblinking focus at six in the morning, already too much.

I pulled the sheet up to my chest.

"What are you doing?" I asked.

"I made you a smoothie," he said, his voice reaching for cheerful and falling short. "I thought you could use the nourishment."

"Why are you sitting on the floor?"

"I don't know. I figured if I got back in bed, I might disturb you." He held up his hands mockingly.

I eyed him and took the green smoothie anyway. My throat was parched enough to override the fact that I hadn't brushed my teeth yet.

"That's it. Drink up. Get your nourishment. "I told you, you've been looking tired lately. Feeling, okay?"

"I guess. I've been so exhausted, I can't remember the last time I slept peacefully. I'm up, then down. I don't know." I shook my head, wondering how the Valium was still failing me.

"Well, after you drink your breakfast, shower and pull yourself together. Your hair's all over the place. You look terrible, Eve. I'm going for a run, not going into the office today. Think you can do some grocery shopping between meetings?" He popped up from the floor, already dressed.

"Sure."

"Want me to warm the car? Or should I have Tom bring it around?" He walked away without waiting for an answer.

It was a beautiful spring day in New Jersey. Trees had bloomed, done with their winter bareness. Green everywhere—real relief after the long, locked-down pandemic winters we had experienced the years prior. Warm enough for a light jacket but not yet sandals.

I took my time at the store, filled the car carefully, his favorite water, fruits and vegetables for smoothies, and my gardenias. Before I closed the trunk, I stopped to breathe them in. That sweet hint of fragrance. Spring, finally.

Back in the driver's seat, my phone chimed with Cam's notification. A picture of him smiling, caption saying he was thinking about me, missing me. My stomach turned over. His surprise messages always landed in that unexpected and warm way. I missed him more than I usually let myself acknowledge. I texted back and snapped a quick selfie. I never felt like I had to perform for Cam. Never needed to be anything but what I was.

On the road home, I turned the music up and sang along sounding like I was down bad.

"Twin, where have you been? Nobody knows me like you do.

Nobody gon' love me quite like you. Can't even deny it, every time I try it. One look in my eyes, you know I'm lying, lying."

Memories of Cam made my voice sweeter to no one but me.

The supermarket was twenty minutes out. I hoarded that car time—a luxury when my routine was mostly work-from-home and the occasional express bus into the city for in office meetings. I took my exit and that's when it happened. Everything in front of me bent to the right in a bizarre curve. I grabbed the wheel so hard the grooves pressed into my palms. My arms locked. I fought to steer in what I thought was the right direction, shoulders up near my ears, my whole-body rigid.

I hit the brakes hard. Praying I didn't slam into the railing. Horns blew behind me, but I couldn't think past the blur in front of my eyes—I just needed to stop before I hurt someone.

My car jolted to a halt, my head snapping back into the headrest, and like that, my vision cleared. Cars flew past. A man slowed down, mouthed something at me, gave me the finger, pulled off, his blond hair whipping in the velocity.

I sat there panting, both hands still on the wheel. I'd never felt anything like it. Pure terror, both for myself and whoever might have been in my path. I turned off the music—the blaring of it suddenly unbearable. Put my hands over my eyes and just breathed.

A knock on my window made me jump.

I rolled it down.

"Are you okay? You were swerving. Is everything all right?" A handsome man peered in.

"Uh. I think I'm fine. I just felt lightheaded for a moment. Really,

I'm fine now. Thank you."

"Are you sure? Perhaps I should call 911. You really shouldn't be on the road if you're feeling lightheaded."

"No, I'm really okay. It wasn't so bad. It lasted about five seconds. Besides, I live less than five minutes up the road. I think I can make it home."

"I'm not trying to be weird. I'm a physician at Hackensack University Medical, down the street. I want you to be safe. If you're saying you live close, okay. I'll still tail you for a bit, especially since you only live five minutes away. It's in the direction I was going in anyway. Even if you think you're feeling better, you should see your primary care provider soon. If it happens again, you might not be so lucky. Take care." Dr. McDreamy tapped my hood before walking away.

I watched him in my side mirror as he went back to his late-model sports coup. He paused before opening his door, glancing back toward my car like he knew I was watching. He flashed me a quick smile and got in. He waited for me to pull off.

I smiled too, despite just having had the scariest five seconds of my life. I looked at my purse in the passenger seat. You may need to let that habit go. The little relaxation pills. I decided right then and there—no more Valium unless I actually needed it, for travel, not for managing Sebastian on a Tuesday. Not recreationally.

I pulled off and made it home, grateful in a way that sat quietly in my chest.

As I pulled into the garage, I texted Sebastian. He came down to help with groceries. I must have looked worse than I realized—when I came around to the back of the car, something crossed his face that I couldn't quite name. His eyes found my shaking hands and lit up with something that looked almost like satisfaction before he composed himself into a look that feigned concern.

"Are you okay, babe? You're shaking like a leaf!" He clasped my hands between his.

"I think I'm okay. You wouldn't believe what just happened... I was on my way home and got so dizzy. I couldn't see the road clearly for a few seconds. Everything was moving right then left. It was so frightening!"

"You're going to lie down as soon as you get upstairs. I'm making you tea and preparing dinner tonight. I want you to rest."

Sebastian's nurturing side was rare enough to be remarkable. I soaked it up.

"I should probably make an appointment with my doctor soon. I'm scared to get behind the wheel again."

"I'll schedule with Dr. Porter to see if he has anything open this week or next. I want you to relax." His lips grazed my hairline feeling like a dry leaf.

- ✧ -

The coffee was already brewing when Sebastian came in with a tray—the smell cutting through the headache still throbbing behind my eyes. I hadn't felt him leave the bed. The linens beside me were stone cold by the time I reached for him. He was already fully dressed for work.

"I thought the caffeine might help," he said, setting the tray on my nightstand. "You were out cold."

"Thanks, honey. I must've passed out early last night. Last thing I remember is sipping the tea you made. I didn't get any work done yesterday or even eat dinner. Didn't realize I was that tired."

"I think you were shaken up from your driving scare. When you came down from your adrenaline rush, your body crashed. Not to be funny." He raised his hands in surrender, and chuckled.

"I guess." I shook my head, trying to clear the fog still clinging to the edges of everything.

"Well, eat and drink up. You need your strength. I have to run, babe, but I'll see you tonight. We have leftovers." He leaned over and pressed that cold, dry kiss to my hairline.

It always felt like that. Like touching something that had been left in the refrigerator.

Before I could respond, Sebastian was out the door, already calling back without turning around.

"Don't work too hard today!"

I took the day off. Texted the head of my unit—not feeling well. No

Zoom or Teams, no stock market, no express bus, no city. I texted Justin to say I wouldn't see him at Starbucks.

The cute doctor who'd followed me home crept into my head. I pushed it right back out. Really, Eve? What were you going to do with him after? You need to slow down with all this. Cam is more than enough.

I lay in bed staring at the ceiling, noticing for the first time the tiny shiny flecks in the paint. I thought about the alternate version of yesterday where I didn't get the wheel back in time. Sat with that for a minute. I felt genuinely grateful—for the breath in my chest, for Tom the Bellman holding the door, for the bed I was currently wasting a day off in.

I texted my grandma to tell her I loved her and then showered. I made myself fresh coffee from the Keurig—Sebastian's was still sitting cold on the nightstand. I stepped out onto the balcony and inhaled deeply.

Then, inexplicably, I decided I wanted to do something nice for my husband.

Wash-and-go on my natural curls with some curling cream. I almost picked up the flat iron out of habit — Sebastian had made clear, in the way he made most things clear, that he found my natural hair "a little much." He'd never said it mean, just said it like a fact, the way he said most things he meant to be mean. But I put the iron down. I was going to see him at his office, not perform for him. Dark oversized shades and out the door.

Sebastian's office sat on the ground floor of a contemporary Newark building, twenty minutes from home. The neighborhood was mid-revival—scaffolding and new signage where vacant lots used to be. After a brief stint at a large tech firm, Sebastian had gone into business with a college friend. Whitmore & Robles, information security, a few years old now and growing—ten employees, projecting twenty within five years. I was proud of what he'd built, whatever else I felt about him.

The receptionist looked up as I walked in.

"Hi, Nicole! It's been a while."

"Hi, Ms. Eve. It's been a long time." She seemed to force a smile, and she'd lost at least two shades of color.

"Oh, I remember now! You had a baby recently, didn't you?"

"Yes, she's six months already." She said warmly.

"That's sweet. I'm going to see Sebastian. I want to surprise him, take him to lunch." I started toward the back.

"Let me call Mr. Whitmore, let him know you're here."

I waved without looking back. "Don't bother."

I got to Sebastian's office and pushed the door open without knocking.

Perfume hit me first. Baccarat Rouge, heavy and deliberate. Then I saw her—still with her back to me, a long jet-black braided ponytail cascading just above her ass, body poured into a skintight black skirt. She'd positioned herself on the edge of his desk, so he had a direct sight up it.

When she turned, Sebastian's expression cracked wide open before he got it under control.

"Honey, what are you doing here?" He chuckled, rubbing his chin.

"Interrupting your meeting, am I?" I fixed my gaze on the unfamiliar, very pretty face.

She shifted, tugging the skirt down like it had traveled up on its own. Button-up blouse with the top three buttons open, double-D situation, chest highlighted with what looked like Rihanna's body lava.

Vibrant red lips for a midweek afternoon, interesting.

"Uh, honey, this is Jada Jennings. New manager of sales." Sebastian barely got it out, desire still visible around the edges of his composure.

My eyebrow moved on its own. Manager of sales, sure.

Jada looked me up and down. I returned it. She broke first—then spoke.

"Call me JJ. Nice to meet you. Evelyn, or is it, Eva? Right?" She turned back to Sebastian, smirk already in place.

"Eve," I said, dry as sand, eyes staying on Sebastian. "When did she start?"

"I started about six months ago, Eva," Jada said, finally retracting the hand I'd left hanging. I wasn't shaking that bitch's hand.

The audacity.

"I stopped by with hopes of taking you to lunch. But it seems you may already be full." I let that sit.

Something was off in that room from the first second—the ease between them, the way she hadn't flinched when I walked in.

"You should've called. Perhaps I can shift some things around for you, and we can make it happen," Sebastian said, that nervous chuckle making its third appearance.

I looked briefly at his crotch. "No. I think you've done enough shifting for the day. I'll see myself out and see you at home." I rolled my eyes at both of them and walked out.

“It was nice to meet you, Evelyn.” Jada said to my back.

As I got close to the door, Jada's sarcastic goodbye caught me. I turned right back around.

"Unfortunately, I can't say the same, Jade. Funny, Sebastian never mentioned you, but I guess he only talks about hires that are important to the company," I said, deliberately mispronouncing her name like she had several times with mine, staring her in eyes. I wanted to do more, like choke the snotty bitch. I stopped myself, walked away, and left the door wide open.

"Goodbye, Eve. It was good seeing you again," echoed behind me as I moved past Nicole and out through the glass doors.

I walked fast. Mild embarrassment on top of the anger—he'd made a spectacle of me in front of people who knew my name. He called after me, and I moved faster. Then his fingers found my wrist.

"Ughh! What the hell are you grabbing my wrist for? Let go of me!" I yanked my arm back.

Sebastian's face smoothed into something patient and pitying. He reached out like he was steadying me. Close enough that I could smell that morning's coffee on his breath.

"Eve, look at yourself. You're making a scene in front of the staff," he said, dropping his voice into that soft, therapeutic register. "I'm worried that stress is getting to you. I think you're confused."

"Stress? You're chasing me through your company parking lot while Miss Black corporate Barbie sits and watches from your office window!" I snapped.

"Enough! You know I don't do this ratchet shit. I don't," Sebastian said, voice dropping, eyes scanning the lot.

"Let's be civil. You know I love you dearly. It's all just a misunderstanding. Jada is creative, and she's brilliant. She's brought so much to the company in terms of knowledge. So, I don't know what you thought you saw, but it isn't what you think," Sebastian insisted, performing conviction.

He thought he was persuasive. He wasn't. I'd been around enough smoke to smell a fire.

"Yeah, okay, Sebastian," I said, and grabbed my car door handle.

"I'll see you at home for dinner, my sweet," Sebastian said, pressing a kiss to my hairline before walking back toward his building, hands in his pockets, practically bouncing.

I got in the car and didn't start it. I just sat there, watching him skip back to work like he'd won something. I hit the steering wheel until my right arm screamed at me to stop.

Office flirtations happened. Work spouses existed. But that woman had walked in knowing exactly who she was to my husband—her body language said it before her mouth could. She hadn't come for a job.

Back home, I put Sebastian's casserole in the oven and booked an appointment with my primary—a few weeks out, there weren't any appointments available sooner. I fought the urge to text Cam, I started and deleted three messages, then gave up and opened his Instagram just to look at him.

The first picture stopped me cold. A curly-haired, brown-skinned girl with a wide smile, standing next to Cam at the airport in Jamaica.

"We're here!"

I closed the app and unfollowed him. Turns out I wasn't just keeping a side piece. I was someone else's.

Chapter 5

DIGITAL GHOSTS

Hello," I answered, already rolling my eyes as Kiki's voice came through bright and loud. I'd just stepped out of the office for my weekly on-site day. My lunch hour was not meant for this.

"Hey, girl! I called to invite you and Sebastian for dinner in a few weeks. We'll have a few friends over to celebrate Lance's promotion. He just became a partner at the firm," she squealed, voice jumping an octave.

"Oh, that's great!" I meant it. Lance had bled for that firm, built his client list from scratch, let the work do the talking. He'd earned it.

"I'll talk to Sebastian and let you know. Hopefully, we can make it."

"Hopefully? Excuse me, cousin. I'm like your sister; I need you there to celebrate with us. It really won't be the same without you guys. Besides, I have some new pieces I just got in from Milan that I want to show you. Mali and all the girls will be there. You can't miss it!" Kiki gushed.

"Shit!" My heel got caught in a crack on the pavement.

"Listen, Kiki, I have to go." I wanted off this call.

"Okay, but wait, I need to come by and get the Ginger Brown pen shell tray you borrowed from me a few months ago."

"Sure. It's in the cabinet over the sink. Come whenever you like; you still have a copy of the key card, right?" I sighed, already anticipating the lecture on proper finish care. She'd probably need it to anchor the spread for her next event.

"Perfect! I'll be there in the next week or so to pick it up. If you can... be a gem and leave it on the counter for me so that I don't have to go rummaging through the Sebastian's perfectly organized cabinets, that would be great."

"Kiki? I'll leave it out. I must go. Ciao!" I ended the call.

At my desk, working through a salad, I pulled up LinkedIn and searched Jada Jennings. Something had been needling me since the office visit. I wanted her employment history before she walked into Sebastian's company.

Nothing. Not a trace.

My heart rate started beating fast and loud, the kind of pounding I could feel in my ears. I looked up from my screen and the glass walls of my office felt unfamiliar, the whole floor suddenly went off kilter. I breathed through it, hands shaking despite the effort. A coworker passed by and I said nothing. After a few minutes, my heart settled. I texted Bella and Justin that I'd meet them for happy hour. I needed to get out of my own head.

"Chick, what's gotten into you? Or rather, who? You don't seem like yourself," Bella said as we settled in, waiting for Justin.

"What? I look how I feel, huh?" I wasn't answering until

Justin arrived.

I spotted him navigating the suited-up crowd—more frayed than usual, dabbing his forehead with a napkin as he dropped into the chair.

"Wow, this place is packed for a Tuesday, Rona aint been gone that long it's still lurking about. But not for New Yorkers, they are lushes, damn," Justin panted. "If one more junior associate tries to 'circle back' on a brief I finished days ago, I am going to scream. My boss is riding me, Eve, and Marcus is barely speaking to me because I'm never home for dinner anymore. I feel like I'm failing at everything at once."

I reached out and patted his hand. "I'm sorry, Jus. You're just overworked. It'll pass."

He took a breath, tried to shake it off as the waiter appeared. "But enough about my tragic life. Why the long face? Sister over here looking like she needs some dick," Justin said, as he glanced at Bella for backup.

"Well, I could always use some dick," I said, trying to keep it light. "But that's not what's wrong. I think Sebastian is messing with this chick at the office, making me look stupid. It's one thing to cheat but he should know better than to shit where he eats."

Bella's eyes widened. "What do you mean, you think? What makes you think that?" She glanced at Justin, who was nursing his martini with perfect composure.

"I went to his office to take him to lunch, and I found this chick perched on his desk. Skirt damn near up around her waist. Bash was all into her, too, like he was getting high off the scent of her pussy. He looked like he saw a ghost when he saw me, and she had the nerve to try and talk slick. She wanted me to know I walked in on their little office situation."

"And you, missy? You didn't drag this chick?" Justin peered at me over the rim of his glass.

"I was at his company. The place he's put his blood, sweat, and tears into. I couldn't go in there acting up, but I wanted to. Trust me, it took everything in me not to slap Bash and this bitch." I sighed, frustration evident in my voice.

Bella gave a flurry of blinks and a sharp smirk. "Well, the Eve I knew is gone and has been replaced by this new nice Eve. In your heyday, well... never mind. You know how we used to get down," she laughed, sticking her tongue out.

"Did you say anything to Sebastian about how you're feeling?" Justin's voice went serious.

"I sure did. He told me I was being silly and that she's a good employee and all that baloney. But something doesn't seem right. You all know I know when it's more than just a business relationship."

"We know you know! So, what's the biggie if he's messing with her a little something? It's not like he's going to leave you. Or is she that damn fine?" Justin gave a dry laugh.

"She's pretty, voluptuous. She looks like one of those reality TV chicks. Big tits, inflated ass, flat belly, and airbrushed makeup. I guess most straight men would be attracted to her."

"Well, where's she from?" Bella wondered.

"I don't know. I tried to look her up on LinkedIn since Sebastian said she was an asset to the company, but I couldn't find anything."

"LinkedIn? Sis, are you serious? If you want the down and dirty, we need to find her social media pages, not some damn work social media!" Justin scoffed before continuing. Justin offered as he pulled out his phone and navigated to the various social media sites.

After searching a few pages of Jada Jennings, we found her on Instagram and Facebook her page was not private, which Justin called a gift. He slid the phone across the bar to me without comment. Her profile picture was an eye-catching picture of her in a bright two-piece orange bikini. We clicked on her profile and were surprised that her page was open to the world's view. Bella leaned close to Justin and me to look at the woman who seemed to have my husband's attention.

"She's okay, but she's not you." Bella's hand brushed my arm as we scrolled through the pictures.

"I find it odd. A beautiful woman like this, and no man? Not in any pictures?" Justin stroked his chin with exaggerated gravity.

Justin zoomed in on something, his expression sharpening. "Actually — hold on. Facebook's got one." He turned the screen. There was Jada at what looked like a wedding reception — not hers, someone else's — standing beside a broad-shouldered man with a close cut and a jawline like a sculpture. A tagged comment underneath read: Jada & Derek always couple goals ❤.

"She's married," Bella said flatly.

Justin looked at me. "And you're married. And Sebastian I put money on it knows her from way, way back." He put the phone down and picked up his drink. "That's a very tight little circle, baby."

I said nothing. I just filed it away — Derek, the husband, the face I'd never seen before — and kept scrolling.

The account was curated the way people curate things when they want to be seen living well — travel shots, rooftop dinners, the occasional motivational caption. I scrolled slowly, not sure what I was looking for.

Then Justin reached over and took the phone back, tapping through something. "Look at this." He turned the screen toward me again. It was a Facebook page, older, the profile photo a different version of the woman I'd met — younger, college-age, the braids shorter. And there, in a tagged photo from what the timestamp placed at over fifteen years ago, was a face I recognized immediately.

Sebastian. Younger, jaw softer, wearing a football jersey with a number I didn't recognize. His arm was around Jada. They were both laughing at something outside the frame, and the comfort between them was the kind you don't manufacture — the kind that comes from years of knowing exactly how someone stands.

The caption read: Bowie High Homecoming, forever my girl.

I put the phone down on the bar.

"Bowie," Bella said. "That's Maryland."

"Sebastian grew up in Maryland," I said. My voice came out even, which surprised me.

Justin picked the phone back up and kept scrolling. More photos surfaced as he dug deeper, the way old social media always did when you went looking — prom photos, graduation photos, the scattered digital residue of a whole relationship that had existed before I'd ever entered the picture. Jada in a yellow dress. Sebastian in a rented tux with his arm around her waist. Both of them bright and easy in each other's company.

"They were prom king and queen," Justin said, holding up a photo.

"I genuinely cannot make this up."

I stared into my glass and turned the straw in my fingers. The question moved through me in slow circles. Why would he keep her a secret? It wasn't that it was just an affair, if that's what it was — the history. The years. The fact that she had existed in his life long before I had, that she had a name and a context and that told me she had been briefed about me as a formality.

"Five years," I said. "He never mentioned her once."

"Not once?" Bella asked.

"Not a name, not a city, nothing. He told me he didn't date much in high school. That he was focused on school. I'm sure I mentioned Cam to him as my high school sweetheart, at least in passing early in our relationship." I heard how it sounded as I said it. The story he'd given me — clean, simple, designed to leave no threads worth pulling.

Justin set the phone face-down on the bar. "Baby," he said, "that's not a woman he forgot to mention. That's a woman he buried."

We sat with that for a moment. The bar noise moved around us, indifferent.

"What are you going to do?" Bella asked.

I didn't have an answer. I had the photographs and the timeline and a husband who had looked me in the eye two days ago and said she'd come highly recommended. I had the cold, specific feeling of a story that had been happening around me without my knowledge, a whole parallel geography I hadn't been given access to.

He tried to frame it as if they were just co-workers. I knew they seemed more comfortable than just two people who worked together," I huffed.

"Well, she looks like a chick that goes after what she wants. Look at the look in her eyes. She did not come to play, Sis. You better get in Sebastian's ass and find out what's happening. Well, not in his ass.

Well, then again, maybe." Justin's laugh was a sharp, mocking bark.

He raised his martini and took a pointed sip through the tiny straw.

I knocked back my cocktail in one long swallow and flagged the waitress for another.

I stared into the empty glass and twirled the straw absentmindedly. Why would he keep her a secret? The question circled tighter each time. Indignation and something hollow underneath it.

Bella leaned in, eyes narrowing. "Well apparently there's some ancient history between them, and he's not eager to reveal that his former flame is now under his employment."

"Perhaps," I said, "but I'll unravel this mystery when I'm back home. No need for him to weave a web of deception around me."

Justin elbowed my arm. "Didn't he though, Miss Thing? You were not ready to hear that he's clocking in with his ex. Come on now, Sissy." His hand came down on mine, a steady weight.

"Whatever, Jus. Here's the deal. If you bring your ex on board, either you're keeping the past on the hush-hush for a reason, or there's still some unfinished business. I don't know, but her vibe? Something's off."

"Sis, I recommend a couple more sips before you confront

Sebastian's rigid ass self," Justin advised, flagging down the waitress once again. As the night unfolded, I was feeling a bit tipsy and ready for a liberating escape. Contemplating a message to my favorite macaroni stirrer, Cam, I grimaced at the reminder of his current travel escapade with his boo-thang. With a disappointed sigh, I headed home to what masqueraded as my life.

Coming through the door, I found Sebastian on the balcony, glass door pulled shut, back turned, deep in a conversation I couldn't hear. But I could see him. The man was electric—pacing, nodding in sharp decisive jerks, AirPods in, both hands free to conduct some invisible orchestra. Then he doubled over laughing and as he straightened up, he locked eyes with me through the glass and all the laughing stopped.

The call seemed to have ended abruptly at the sight of me. He lingered on the balcony, staring out at the city lights like he was deep in thought.

My first instinct was to go to him, rub his shoulders, offer him something tender, some affection maybe, and in return, maybe he would offer an apology about Jada that I could believe. Instead, I went to the bath and soaked, hoping whatever mood he was in would carry over into something gentler later.

The jazz came first, bright and invasive, before I was even fully awake—Sebastian in a good mood was a whole ass event. He appeared in the doorway to brush my hairline while I was still tying my robe.

"Rise and shine, sleeping beauty. Freshen up, brush your teeth, and join me for a delightful breakfast."

I braced myself against the vanity and waited for the shots

from last night to stop making their final case against me standing upright. Once I looked roughly human, I made my way to the dining area.

"I've prepared your favorites, red-skinned potatoes, these vile bird placenta eggs, swine delicacy, and a generous serving of carbs."

I made a face. "Thanks, I guess. You sure know how to make a girl hungry."

Sebastian chuckled. "I'm just pulling your leg, honey. I know you indulge in animal flesh every now and then. Although, if you keep enjoying this stuff, those last ten pounds might decide to stick around for the long haul. But hey, if it makes you happy, it's all good." He pressed his dry ass lips to my forehead.

I looked at the plate and did the math. He'd made me breakfast and then made me think twice about eating it. Signature Sebastian.

"Why cook all of this? Why not make me a smoothie like you usually do?" I pushed a potato around with my fork. My appetite was somewhere else entirely.

"I thought a hearty meal would help soak up some of the alcohol from your after-work escapade last night. You looked exhausted when you came in, your eyes were vacant, and the scent of alcohol on your breath was so bad it made its way out there." He gestured toward the balcony.

"I wasn't that drunk, Sebastian. I wanted to talk to you about the other day," I said.

Sebastian raised his hand. "We need to talk about your office, Bash.

Is something going on with you and Jada, or whatever her

name is?"

Sebastian's frustration escalated as he expressed, "I thought we moved past this. I forgave you for your reaction the other day, and now you're dredging it up again. I anticipated a pleasant day, but it seems that's not the case. You know what? I went to the fridge this morning to start preparing breakfast and a hot beverage for you to wake up to. What do I see when I open the fridge? I had to turn the creamers around to see which one I was reaching for. Do you think that's fair? I should've been able to easily read which flavor without manually turning the container. But no. You're sloppy, and this, this is what I must deal with. Yet you're questioning me?"

With a forceful push, he distanced himself from the table and rose to his feet.

"You. You are utterly disrespectful! You claim to be a wife, yet you invade my office, my place of business!" Sebastian jabbed a finger at his own chest.

"I won't allow you to drag me into that space, Eve. I won't. If you can't comprehend that two individuals of opposite sexes can work together professionally, that says something about you!" Sebastian's eyes widened and darkened with anger, leaving an intense atmosphere in the room.

"Sebastian! She was sitting on your desk; her skirt was practically around her waist. What's professional about that? Her top didn't look professional. What were you two discussing that she needed to perch on your desk with her vagina practically in your face?"

Sebastian's voice sharpened into a blade. "You're being absurd! I don't know what you think you saw, but it wasn't like that!"

"I'm not being absurd, Bash! Do you know Jada outside of

work? Did you know her before you hired her?" The intensity of the questioning reflected the gravity of the situation, and I wanted to see how far he was going to go with this.

Sebastian chuckled and shook his head, somewhere between a laugh and composing his next lie.

Sebastian threw his head back and huffed, a sound of pure disbelief escaping him. "You're something else, Eve. Are you stalking her?" He waved his finger as if unraveling a mystery. "Is that it? Are you okay? Because this is insane!" He threw his hands up in anger as if struggling to comprehend the intensity of the situation.

"Are you fucking kidding me? Do you know this bitch or not? I'm not stupid, Bash! Apparently, you think I am, though."

Sebastian's eyes went wide, brows down, mouth turning hard, he was almost unrecognizable. He pointed and stepped towards me.

"Lower your damn voice, Eve! Don't you dare accuse me with that tone, not now, not ever! It's about time you seek help for these outbursts. First, at my job, and now this. What's next, Eve?"

I stepped back and held my ground. The air in the room felt heavy.

"What's next? How about the truth, Sebastian? Are you messing with her or not? You didn't just pick her resume off Indeed!" I rose from the table, head suddenly throbbing. Sebastian reached out and caught my wrist—one pull, one cold hand on my shoulder, and pressed me back into the seat. I stared down at his hand.

"I have nothing else to say, Bash. Please let me go. If you claim it's all work, then so be it." My head felt strange, foggy and

I was dizzy. The fight drained the little bit of energy I had out of me. I looked up at Sebastian and thought I was seeing two of him.

"Why are you looking at me like that, Eve? Are you okay?" Something in his eyes that might have been concern—or something else.

He released my wrist. I covered my eyes with both hands, trying to pull the room into focus. "I'm fine. I feel a little dizzy."

"All the arguments have caught up to you. Look at what you've done to yourself with this nonsense. You need to calm down and figure out why you've been having these spells. Running with your friends and excessive drinking, it's taking a toll on you. How about lying down for a nap? I've got to hit the gym. We can discuss communication later when I'm back. Sound good?"

Sebastian didn't wait for my response. He retreated to the bedroom in a deliberate, unhurried silence. I stood in the doorway and watched him lay a shirt across the bed, smoothing the cotton with the flat of his palm until every crease disappeared. He folded it with military precision. "You're having a breakdown, Eve," he said, voice low and terrifyingly calm. "The paranoia, the drinking; you're losing your mind it seems. We need to get you seen by someone before this goes any further." He tucked the square of fabric into his bag and zipped it shut.

The energy went out of me all at once. I made it to the bed and lay down.

My phone buzzed under my pillow almost immediately.

Bella: Hey, Sis, checking on you. I hope you're ok. Call me!

I tried to respond. My mind wouldn't. I was somewhere far off, unreachable. I pushed the phone back under the pillow and let sleep take me.

Chapter 6

ROOTS AND REALITIES

I sipped my coffee and watched Bash scroll through his phone, offering me tight lipped smiles as he typed back messages. It had only been a week since the whole thing with Jada, and he'd been the perfect attentive husband ever since. The façade, we both knew it was that.

My friends had done the digging. The verdict: Jada Jennings and Sebastian Whitmore were high school sweethearts. No more pictures of them together on her page, I guess he had her delete them, but the mutual friends told the story—the "it" couple, prom king and queen, comments full of fairy tale nostalgia. Sebastian's finsta had liked all of them.

I'd had affairs. None of them threatened anything real. Sebastian could be cold, controlling, cruel at the edges—but I'd never pictured a future with any of those men, not even Cam, who'd once been everything to me. The affairs were physical, compartmentalized. Exit hatches, not destinations so I thought.

Jada was different.

She was Sebastian's first love. Maybe his real one.

"I'm taking a few days off," I said, looking at his face.

Bash didn't look up. "Sounds good, honey."

I needed to think. Maybe it was a fling and nothing more, uncomfortable, but survivable. My gut said otherwise. Whatever he had with his prom queen went down to the roots. And I didn't like where that left me standing.

I circled my old block three times before I found a spot. I took a minute just to sit in the car and look. Sakura petals from the cherry blossoms covered the sidewalk. The main street moved with its usual energy—cars, buses, and people carrying on about their day.

I looked up the block and let the memories come. Kiki and I running up and down, her long bushy ponytails bouncing as we played tag with Bella. Summer evenings with ice cream from the ice cream truck, talking about cute boys and back-to-school outfits, block parties. The scent of Grandma's fried chicken floating out the window when it was time to come in. Saturday mornings with incense burning and Kashif or Keith Sweat on the speakers while we did chores—Grandma's R&B; curriculum, early and non-negotiable.

I saw a young, smooth-faced Cam walking me home from school, our hands locked until we hit my stoop, where he always let go—Grandma Locust watched from the parlor window, and he knew better.

I couldn't wait to see her. I always left that house feeling like myself again.

I pushed the gate open and heard her rush to the window.

"Girl, you didn't tell me you were coming, but I should've known. I dreamt about you last night. Get in here and let me see you." She shut the window.

I climbed the steep stairs and found her already at the door.

"I have my key, Grandma. You didn't have to come to the door."

Her locs fell just above her waist—she'd stopped cutting her hair the day my mother passed and hadn't touched it since. Four-eleven of smooth chocolate skin, just like my Mama's. She pulled me in and I breathed her in—sweet cinnamon scent—and felt the whole week's tension leave my shoulders.

"I'll be right back. I'm going to smoke this cigarette right quick. I have food in the kitchen—go make yourself a plate." She popped a Newport between her lips and headed for the door.

I swallowed the stop-smoking speech. She'd heard it every week for years. Today I gave her a break.

The ceiling in the entryway to the Brownstone was painted a haint blue. Grandma said that was to keep the haints and the restless spirits away. She said that the blue made the spirits think it was water or the sky and so they would pass by our house when they were looking for something to get into.

The kitchen smelled like okra and rice—the Gullah Geechee roots Grandma had brought with her from Beaufort, South Carolina, in the seventies, simmered into everything she cooked. I fixed a plate—rice and black-eyed peas, okra, some collards and stewed chicken—and was halfway through it when she came back in.

"How are you doing, baby?" The heavy, rhythmic Gullah drawl she saved for family.

I smiled, thinking about how Kiki and I used to sit wide-eyed at this table while she told us about the hard times in the South, about Dr. Buzzard and his powers in the spirit realm. She made the supernatural feel as real as the linoleum under our feet.

"I'm okay, Grandma. I just wanted to see you. I took a few days off and figured I'd make good use of it. Do a few things for me, you know?"

She studied my face. Offered tea. Sat across from me at the old wooden table I'd eaten at since I was small. Gave me a moment, then fixed her eyes on me.

"What's going on, Eve? Are things okay with you and that husband of yours? Or is he finally showing you his true colors?" I sighed, started to lie, and stopped. She knew.

"Things are weird. I don't know how to explain it."

"Things have always been weird with you two, Eve. What makes them weird now? He was weird when you met him, dated him, accepted his weird marriage proposal... but they're weird now?" Her expression was serious, probing.

"I don't know, Gram. I just feel like I'm in a dark place."

Grandma's face went solemn.

"You know, baby, sometimes you must slip into the darkness to see the light."

I took a deep breath and laid it out—all of it. Grandma listened. Sipped her tea. Nodded. When I finished, she asked me to consider something.

"You ever thought about life without Sebastian? Do you think you two were ever equally yoked, honey? I mean seriously. Because from where I'm sitting, things haven't ever been right with you two. I told you that when I met him. This woman at work, his ex-girlfriend—she's not the issue between you and him. Neither is the stuff you do when you think no one is watching. Baby, there's more to life than material comforts. You deserve happiness, love, a partner who uplifts you in every aspect. If you're drowning, you can't build a life raft with the bricks he's throwing at you."

Her words sat in the air.

"I've been in love and seen women in love, Eve, Real love, where their faces light up and their burdens seem lighter because they share them with someone who cares. I haven't seen that with you and Sebastian. What I see is a weary heart, tired of trying to fit into a mold that was never made for you."

"He takes you on trips, buys you more clothes than you can wear, gifts you gadgets that barely serve a purpose. If that's your definition of him 'taking care' of you, then so be it. Personally, I never desired a man to care for me in that manner. My man was always gentle with me, but he was wise enough not to play games. After your granddaddy pulled the wool over my eyes and broke my heart, I said I wouldn't ever let that shit happen again." She chuckled with a sly smile.

I laughed too, thinking about her history with men. In her time, many had tried. After my grandfather, there was Mr. Lewis—her steady until he passed a few years ago. Owned a dry cleaner and several properties throughout Brooklyn. Emotionally present, financially solid, didn't need her to work herself raw. With his support she'd bought two more rental properties in the neighborhood. That instinct for real estate had planted something in me and was the whole reason I chased an MBA.

"Grams, I know Mr. Lewis treated you right," I added.

"And Sebastian better know not to play with you either. He

avoids crossing paths with me because he knows these old cats around here wouldn't leave a trace of his narrow behind if he dared to play games with you. They may be older, but their roots run deep in these streets."

The laughter faded as the weight of what she'd said settled in. Grandma had always been fierce like this, especially since she felt responsible for how things went down with my mother. She'd shielded Kiki and me a lot, she never stopped.

My eyes were filled with tears. She saw through the whole thing—through every excuse I'd made to hold this marriage together.

"Eve, love shouldn't be a burden. It should be a sanctuary, a place where you find solace. If you're questioning his loyalty, if you feel incomplete, then it's time to reassess what you truly want from life. Sometimes it's necessary to let go of what's holding you back to discover what you truly deserve."

She reached across the table and squeezed my hand.

"I'm not saying it'll be easy, but you're stronger than you realize. You were raised by me! A woman who faced adversity and had to stand tall through it all. It's in your blood to be strong, Evie."

I nodded. Took it in. I was grateful for her, for the old wooden table, for the smell of collards still in the air. She'd weathered her storms and now she was sitting here helping me figure out mine.

The rest of the afternoon we spent watching judge shows and gossiping about Kiki and Lance. Grandma, who didn't warm people easily, had genuine love for Lance. The sun rose and set on that man in her eyes—deservedly. He treated Kiki with reverence, and Grandma respected what that looked like up close.

As I got ready to leave, Grandma pulled me close.

She went to her room and came back with the olive oil bottle that had a block of camphor in it, that oil had been prayed over and blessed by Reverend Lyons. As always before I left, she anointed my head and prayed—the kind of prayer that moves through you rather than over you. When she finished, she looked into my eyes the way she sometimes did, like she was reading something written there.

"Eve, why don't you leave Sebastian while you're still whole? While your mind is intact. The spirit is telling me you should part ways. Something doesn't feel right."

I started to protest. She raised her hand.

"I'll keep praying for you, Evie. But I want you to seriously consider getting yourself together and leaving. You know I have plenty of space here, and I won't be in your way. You can save your money and secure a place of your own. Running from one man to another is not the solution to fixing what's wrong in your life either.

Gather yourself, Eve, and summon the strength to move on."

She held me tight for a moment and let go.

Leaving her always left me with a steadiness, a reminder that I had roots, that there was somewhere I could always return to. Could life without Sebastian be real? I didn't know. But for the first time, I was asking the question out loud.

I was still somewhere in that thought, walking down the block, when a horn cut through the noise and I turned to see who was trying to get my attention.

A late-model BMW truck. And Cam, leaning across the driver's seat with that smile.

"What are you doing, woman?"

"I was just visiting my grandmother. What are you doing on my old block?"

"Just got off work. I'm at a site a few blocks up. New buildings are going up, so I have a lot of heating and cooling systems to install. They're keeping your boy busy. Besides, you know how Brooklyn is, building up everywhere. They'll slide a building anywhere if there's a few square feet." He chuckled.

"They're keeping you busy, huh? So, you're back from your vacation with your girlfriend. You guys looked like you had a good time." I couldn't resist throwing that out there.

Cam sighed before responding, "Listen, Eve, are you in a rush?"

"I have time. Why, what's up?"

"I don't want to sit here and double park, holding up traffic on these narrow blocks. There's a coffee shop around the corner. You know they're popping up like crazy over here. Let me park and meet me around the corner at the little coffee shop with the big blue sign. I forget the name of it, but you can't miss it."

"Okay, cool. I'll see you there in a few minutes."

I walked past Grandma's house and around the corner into the coffee shop that had colonized the block. Sterile and white-tiled, roasted-bean scent doing its best against everything it lacked. Compared to Grandma's kitchen, the steam, the smell of collards, the weight of everything stored in those walls—this place felt like a stage set. All minimalist lines and no memory. I was a daughter of rice and peas and Gullah prayers, and here I was ordering drinks in a space that seemed designed to sand all of that down. I found a corner table, took off my jacket, and sat.

A slim, sandy-haired waitress came over full of energy.

"Two café mochas with an extra shot, foam, whole, and please make it extra hot. Two blueberry muffins toasted, hold the butter. Thanks," I said, quietly amused at how automatic Cam's order had become in my hands.

When Cam walked in, the room shifted. He had that quality, he commanded attention without asking for it. The waitress flushed when she smiled at him. He spotted my wave and came straight over, still in his work clothes: jeans, white tee, Timberlands. He pulled out the chair across from me and sat down grinning, that single dimple and crooked smile doing its work.

"You look good, Eve. I can't believe I ran into you like this. You were visiting Grams, I see."

"Yes, just a drop-by to check in on her. It's like she's checking on me when I go see her," I chuckled.

"I see she anointed your head." Cam pointed to my forehead.

"Oh yeah, can't leave without her doing that."

"And you shouldn't. She knows what she's doing. You've been MIA; I haven't heard from you," Cam remarked.

"I haven't been MIA. I saw you went away with your little girlfriend. Didn't want to bother you. You looked all in love and shit in your IG pictures. Who am I to come in between true love?" I said sarcastically.

Cam pointed at me. "You're funny, Eve. Tia is just a good friend. We date off and on, but it's nothing serious. Besides, I couldn't take you to Jamaica now, could I? I'd prefer you to go any day, but I'm sure your hubby would take issue with that."

The waitress arrived with perfect timing, breaking whatever

had started building between us. "Two extra shots of hot café mochas and two toasted blueberry muffins, dry." She placed them neatly in front of us.

"Thank you." I barely looked up.

"You're welcome. Let me know if I can get you anything else," she said, directing most of it at Cam.

We picked up our drinks at the same time, both holding eye contact over the cups. I broke first.

"Cam, if I weren't married, I'd make more time for you. I enjoy my time with you always. But I'm married to Sebastian."

"I know who you're married to, Evie. Marriage is a choice, though, a choice that you make. You aren't all that happy with old boy."

I rolled my eyes. "You don't know anything about our situation. I don't talk to you about Sebastian, so don't make assumptions about whether I'm happy with him."

"Evie, you fuck me whenever you can, at least you were. That doesn't seem like a happy wife. I say I'm not judging, because I promised I wouldn't when we first started this, but it's a lie. Every time you leave my bed to go back to him, I want to punch a wall. I'm just saying. You know how I feel about you; I don't want you to doubt that.

But you're a married woman, so yes, I have to date; I have to keep myself entertained while you play married."

I bit into my muffin and chewed slowly, buying time. The truth was I needed him and seeing him happy with someone else stung more than I wanted to admit. He wasn't wrong. What right did I have to be upset about Tia?

"You know, Cam, I've been thinking a lot about my situation, and you're right. My behavior doesn't exactly paint the picture of a happily married woman," I confessed.

Cam leaned in, expression settling. "I'm listening."

"I'm not saying I'm leaving him. I'm just evaluating," I offered cautiously.

"Well, you know it's fate that we ran into each other today. You know that, right?" Cam asked.

"Fate, maybe. Coincidence, probably more like it."

"Coincidence? There's no such thing, and things line up as they should," Cam declared.

He had that way about him—always had, even as a kid. We sat there for over an hour, working through the mochas, catching up on everything we'd missed. His laugh. The way he licked his lips between sentences. The way he looked at me like I was worth looking at. I remembered, sitting there, exactly why this had never fully stopped.

I told him I'd reach out soon and we agreed to dinner. If Jada could walk into Sebastian's company as a "colleague," then Cam could be my equivalent. The sun was already down by the time we left, streetlights making everything orange and close. As was his habit outdoors, Cam asked if he could hold my hand. I said yes. His large hand closed over mine, and we walked like that to my car. He opened the door, stood close. Even after a full day of labor, he still smelled faintly of his cologne. He pulled me in. I looked up at him and our lips met, and I let myself sink into it—into him—feeling something I never had to perform or explain or be careful with.

Chapter 7

THE TRUTH IN THE AISLES

Grandma's words were still in my ear on the drive home. That advice sitting on my shoulders like something I couldn't put down.

Kiki, Lance, simpler times—the whole afternoon had been a temporary patch on a leaking pipe. But every turn of the wheel brought Grandma's words back. About Sebastian. About marriage. About leaving before I lost myself entirely.

Leaving Sebastian while I still had my sanity. The idea had once felt impossible. Now it didn't.

When I got back to the apartment, Sebastian was on his phone—animated, laughing that laugh I almost never heard. Same scene as before. He hung up the moment he saw me, offered the same hollow smile, the same lie about Josh from accounting. I didn't challenge it. I'd already stopped believing anything that came out of his mouth. What I was doing instead was watching. Every micro-expression, every time his eyes slid away from mine. It was data. And the data had been telling me something I couldn't ignore anymore.

A few days later I was at the market, trying to feel like a normal person. I paused in the floral section and leaned into a gardenia plant. Impulsively, I dropped it in my cart. A whole room of that smell sounded like exactly what I needed.

In the cereal aisle, reaching for oatmeal, I heard my name.

"Eve, is that you?"

I turned toward the voice, it was Nicole, Sebastian's receptionist.

"Hey, Nicole, what a surprise! Are you off today?" I questioned, not expecting to encounter her in the middle of the day.

Her face went slack, her lashes fluttering. "I don't work with them anymore, Eve. I thought Sebastian might have mentioned it. I was let go shortly after your visit."

That landed wrong. Nicole had been with Sebastian's company since day one.

"I'm sorry to hear this. No, Sebastian didn't inform me. May I ask what happened?"

Nicole smirked. "Do you want the politically correct version or the truth?"

"The truth would be appreciated."

"Do you have a few minutes to talk? I don't want to discuss this in the middle of the cereal aisle."

"I do. I was just about to check out. Why don't you finish your grocery shopping, and I'll meet you at the salad spot next door?"

I rushed through checkout, a knot tightening in my chest. He'd let her go without a word to me, that was odd.

After loading up the car, I settled into a table at the salad bar and waited. Nicole came in with her red hair framing her face, looking slim in a two-piece athletic set, all the baby weight gone.

"So, what happened? I mean, you were like Sebastian's right hand."

Nicole closed her water bottle and looked at me. "She happened. That Jada, the Grinch, happened!" Nicole huffed and rolled her big blue eyes.

"Okay, I see you're not a fan of the fair lady. What happened?"

"So, do you remember the day you came to the office?" Nicole began. "A few minutes after you left, Sebastian called me into his office. Jada was sitting on the side of his desk. Sebastian asked me if letting guests walk into his office without his consent was regular practice."

I stared at her. Was I the guest?

Nicole continued, "I said, but it was Eve. She's your wife. Sebastian was about to say something else when Jada cut him off. 'Nicole, you don't allow guests in without letting Sebastian or me know. This kind of blunder could cost us.' Jada sashayed her way to my desk at the end of the day and handed me a letter terminating my employment. When I tried to speak to Sebastian, she told me he had nothing to say." Nicole's eyes welled up with tears.

"Wow. Well, I don't know if you could tell by how I left the office that day, but of course, I walked in, and they weren't exactly having what I would call a business meeting."

"Yeah, I figured you saw something. The environment has become so toxic since she got there. I'm sorry to tell you this, but I think

Sebastian's having an affair with her."

I sighed. "Unfortunately, I got the hint when I was there that day.

So, what you're telling me is no surprise."

What really stung was the scope of it—Jada calling shots at the office, dismissing my husband's employees, acting like she already had the job I thought I held. That didn't sit right at all. We finished up, and I drove home with the weight of it settling in.

- ✧ -

I needed to put that day somewhere I couldn't feel it for a while. I lit lavender and eucalyptus candles throughout the apartment, showered, put on R&B;, and poured lavender bath oil into the water. The moment I sank in, I felt my shoulders drop.

When I opened my eyes, Sebastian was sitting on the edge of the tub watching me. I almost came out of my skin.

"You act like you've seen a ghost!" he exclaimed.

"I wasn't expecting to see you there." He'd broken my sense of peace just by sitting there.

"Eve, I noticed the brown towels in the linen closet. I'm a bit concerned, they're so dark and somber. I only want the apartment to feel like a sanctuary for you while you're struggling with these moods. Let's stick to the cream ones; they're much better for your mental state."

I was in my Zen. I was not about to let this man insult my towels.

"Sebastian, hold on just a moment." My tone was matter of fact.

"Relax, Eve. Just sit back and relax; I'll be right back."

He came back loosening his tie. "Here, I thought a nice glass of wine would help you relax even more." He raised his eyebrow, handing me the glass.

It was cool in my hand. Exactly what I needed, even with all the bitterness sitting between us. I pressed the glass to my lips and took a long sip. Strawberry and raspberry on my tongue.

"Why didn't you tell me you fired Nicole?"

Sebastian looked away, searching the air for an answer he thought would make sense. "It just wasn't working out with her. It wasn't that serious, Evie. I didn't think you'd care to know."

The wine disappeared in several long, desperate swallows. It hit faster than usual, a wave of heavy relaxation that moved through me before I could track it. Sebastian smirked, ran his hand under the water and up my thigh. My mind said stop, open your mouth and say it, but my body went soft under his hands. My head dropped back against the tub.

"That's it, ree-lax." Each syllable carved out slow and deliberate.

And then I was just tired. Too tired for the orgasm that was coming. My vision blurred at the edges. My body went heavy. I felt the air when he lifted me from the water. The bed. His hands, cool and dry, toweling me off. A surge of something—heat, lust, a laugh that wasn't really mine—and then nothing.

- ✧ -

I woke up to my phone ringing. I blinked at the ceiling, trying to remember where I was.

My body felt like it had been through something. Between my legs, I felt swollen and a stinging pain. I stumbled to the bathroom mirror: a handprint on my shoulder. I stared at it for a long moment, then went back to bed, piecing nothing together.

"Hello," I said, seeing Bash's side of the bed was already empty.

My phone rang and, seeing Grandma's name on the screen, I quickly answered.

"How are you, my dear?" Grandma's voice was laced with worry. "Sebastian called me, saying he was concerned about you. He claims you've been acting off. If he took the time to call me, I wanted to make sure you were okay."

I pressed my hand to my temple. "I'm fine, Grams. The only one acting off is him. He's trying to make me seem crazy because I've been asking about his work friend."

"Well, I hope you've thought more about what we discussed. You'll have your own space here," Grams said before hanging up.

I looked toward the bay window. Dark already. I'd slept the entire day? I pulled on a robe and walked toward the living room. I could hear faint voices.

Jada was there, with a glass of wine lifted to her lips, laughing at something Sebastian said. She turned and looked at me like I'd interrupted her favorite show.

"Oh, honey, you're awake," Sebastian attempted to sound sincere.

"Why is she here?" I demanded.

"Jada was nice enough to stop by and bring me some files," Sebastian explained. "I told her I was thinking of taking off a few days to take care of you, since you had been under the weather."

"You have no business at my house." I moved toward her and Sebastian grabbed me. Jada stood up, looked at me like I was something spoiled and dirty. "I'll hold the office down while you get your wife some help," she said, and let herself out.

When she was gone, he released me. "You're not yourself, Eve. It's this paranoia—it's making you so irrational. I'm only saying this because I love you, but we really need to get you some professional help before you spiral any further."

My palm found his cheek before I could even draw breath. The rage in his eyes sent a chill down my spine. He grabbed my shoulders and slammed me into the wall. "Look at how worked up you've become," he whispered. He leaned in and pressed a ghost of a kiss to my cheek. "I'm going to stay in a hotel for a few nights. I think you need the space to realize how much your behavior is affecting those around you. It's for your own good, darling."

"Sebastian, I think we need to separate," I whispered.

"I love you, Eve, and I'm not going to let you give up on us that easily." His lips brushed my forehead in the same passionless manner as always, and he was gone.

- ✧ -

Later that night I was at Justin's, sitting in his living room with the thick plush carpet under my bare feet. Bella was working through some jerk BBQ lamb chops. Justin was pacing with a scowl, pouring dark liquor into a glass and barely acknowledging I'd walked in. "He's doing it again," he said.

"Marcus thinks he can just go 'radio silent' every time we have a disagreement. I'm thirty-four, Eve. I'm too old to be ghosted by a man I share a lease with." He set the bottle down. "Anyway. Enough about my disaster. You look like you've been through a war."

"I'm going to leave him, and I've decided to quit my job," I said, stopping the music. "I'm not happy at home or with work, and neither is he. He had the nerve to have that Jada chick in my house. My house!"

I watched their eyes widen. "Wait. You're not leaving him because of this Jada chick, are you? She don't get to claim your man, and what the fuck is she doing at y'all house?" Bella asked. "That's your husband, Evie. He got the nerve to bring her to your place. His ass is bold, they both are."

"Yeah, lots of damn nerve, I wanted to hurt them both. Think about this, how often do I invite you two over?" I asked. They exchanged a long, heavy look that filled the space between them. "I don't feel comfortable inviting my best friends to my house because my husband would disapprove. I feel vacant and unloved and I'm tired of it. There's a coldness between us, shits unreal."

"Sebastian is holding onto some coins," Justin offered. "I suggest you consult a good divorce lawyer before telling his ass you're ready to part ways."

"My girlfriend Tara is married to a divorce lawyer. I can get his business card for you," Bella added.

I looked at the wine in my glass. "I'll take that divorce lawyer info; I need to get out soon. That apartment is starting to feel like an asylum."

Chapter 8

THE EXIT STRATEGY

How does one embark on the journey of leaving both her husband and career?

I walked through the high-rise we'd shared for five years—five years, too long. It had always felt more like a showroom than a home, a sprawling sequence of cold rooms I'd soon trade for ground-level Brooklyn. I needed to hold onto every cent.

I stepped out onto the balcony, closed my eyes, breathed in the city. When I opened them, Bash was at the balcony door, watching me.

"Why are you always just watching me? And what are you doing home?" I set my jaw tight.

"Can't I look at my wife? Why is that a problem?" That polished, mocking tilt of his head.

"It's weird. You're always lurking somewhere, watching. Announce yourself. It's strange, Sebastian."

I brushed past him into the sunken living room.

"Funny. You used to think it was cute when I watched you sleep.

Not anymore, huh? Now it's strange, Evie?" He followed me.

"It doesn't feel the same. Maybe it was cute back then, or maybe I didn't know any better. But please stop. I don't like it."

Sebastian laughed a loud laugh when there wasn't shit that was funny.

"Eve, you may need therapy if the simple act of your husband looking at you has become a transgression."

I stared at him. Silence was the only response to a logic I no longer recognized. "You play games with me, Sebastian. You hired your ex at the company. You fired Nicole because your girl didn't like her. And I need therapy? Yes, maybe I do after being married to you."

He chuckled. "The mental problems you have, you came into our marriage with, Eve. Your abandonment issues with your mother. Your ghost daddy troubles. Growing up in that bad neighborhood. It's all affected the wife you are to me. I've done my best to be there for you and will continue to. I'll go to therapy with you. How about that?"

I laughed despite myself, looking at his face for any trace of self-awareness.

"You've got a lot of fucking nerve. But why am I surprised? You had your side bitch sitting in my living room. How about you give me space to figure out the next steps? Take some time away from the apartment. You can come back home in a few days. I should be out by then."

Sebastian studied my face, then patted my shoulder like a colleague. Nothing else. He grabbed a few extra things, dropped them into his packed bag, and walked out.

The apartment breathed when he left. I picked up my phone and called Grandma and told her I'll be home within the week.

Chapter 9

A HOLLOW TRUCE

On the bus ride into the city, I rehearsed my resignation. I'd quit before—always first thing in the morning, always with ritual. This time it felt different. Final.

Sebastian's texts came in waves: love, apologies, flowers. He wanted to fix it. He suggested a marriage counselor, dinner at the Hoboken W to talk it through.

I agreed, though I almost didn't. I needed to tell him face-to-face that we were done. I owed him that—or I told myself I did.

The restaurant was all glass and the kind of steel-and-light elegance that used to mean something to me. I was reading a text from Cam when Sebastian pulled out his chair. Smiling at my phone without thinking.

"That wasn't from me," he said. "Who was that?"

"A friend sent me something funny," I lied smoothly.

He looked at me. "You look beautiful. I love your hair like that."

I knew the style the second he said it. Jada's signature slick back ponytail. My skin crawled at the thought because it wasn't my intention to have my hair look like hers.

"Listen, Sebastian. I agreed to this because I thought I owed you an explanation. But I don't. Not after what you did. I'm not changing my mind. We need to be apart. Whether that's temporary or permanent, I don't know yet. But you know what this is."

He raised his hand, asking me to wait. When he spoke, his voice was different—softer, stripped of its usual control.

"I'm not here to fight. I just need you to consider us before filing for divorce. That's all I'm asking."

For the first time in months, he looked vulnerable. I nodded, said I'd think about it, and we ordered food we barely touched. We talked about the news, about nothing. When he asked if he could come by for more of his things, I said yes.

By the end of the night, something had shifted—not fixed, but quieter. Less like a war, more like a transition. Walking out, I thought maybe this could end without destroying us both. Maybe.

Chapter 10

THE UNRAVELING

The apartment felt different when I got back. Colder. I kicked off my heels and poured a glass of wine, holding onto whatever fragile quiet the dinner had given me. It didn't last.

My phone buzzed. Unknown number.

Unknown: We need to talk. Tomorrow. 2 p.m. Starbucks on Fulton.

Come alone.

My stomach dropped. I knew before the second text came through.

Unknown: It's Jada. Don't make me come to you.

I stared at the screen. Part of me wanted to delete it, block the number, act like I'd never seen it. But I was tired of running. Tired of being the woman things happened to. I wanted to look her in the eye and maybe even claw her shits out.

Fine. 2 p.m.

I didn't sleep. Every time I closed my eyes I saw Sebastian's face at dinner, that vulnerable look, the possibility of a clean ending. Jada's text had torched that. There was nothing civil about any of this.

By morning I'd rehearsed about twelve versions of what I'd say to her. Everyone sounded either too weak or too aggressive. I kept turning it over anyway — the way you run your tongue over a sore tooth, compulsively, uselessly. I finally told myself out loud what I'd been circling all night: you don't have to perform strength. You just have to be honest. I didn't know yet if I believed that.

At 1:45 I walked into the Starbucks on Fulton. Lunch rush—laptops, students, the hiss and grind of espresso machines. My eyes found the back corner.

She sat with her perfect posture, makeup immaculate. Cream blazer, silk blouse, that sleek bun Sebastian had once complimented. When our eyes met, she didn't smile. She gestured to the chair across from her.

I ordered nothing. I wasn't there for coffee.

"Thank you for coming." Her voice was smooth, controlled. "I wasn't sure you would."

"What do you want?" I kept my voice steady, even though my heart was loud.

She sipped her latte, watching me over the rim. "I want to clear the air. This situation has gotten... messy. And I think we both deserve better than the narrative that's being created."

"The narrative?" I leaned forward. "You mean the truth? That you've been sleeping with my husband?"

"It's more complicated than that."

"Is it?" My voice climbed. A few people glanced over. I brought it back down. "Because from where I'm sitting, the lines are clear. You're married to Derek. I'm married to Sebastian. And somehow, you two decided that it didn't matter."

Jada's expression didn't change. "Sebastian and I have history. We were together long before you came into the picture."

That's when it all clicked. Jada was the one he'd never stopped wanting—the thing he wasn't willing to lose even when he had to choose. The plan to marry me was exactly that: a plan. Something to keep his parents satisfied while he kept his real life running in the background.

"Then why didn't he marry you?"

Something flickered across her face—pain or anger, hard to tell which. "His parents didn't approve. My father and his father had a falling out. Business went south, trust evaporated. They threatened to cut him off if he didn't end things with me."

"So, he chose money over you."

"He chose survival," she corrected. "And I understood that. I married Derek because it made sense—for my family, for business.

But Sebastian and I never stopped loving each other."

Something cold and sick moved through me. "And I was what? A placeholder? A convenient wife while he figured out how to get back to you?"

"You were a choice he made under pressure." Her voice softened. That edge of pity was worse than cruelty. "I'm not saying it's fair to you, Eve. I'm just saying it's the truth."

"The truth," I repeated. Their truth tasted bitter in my

mouth. "The truth is that you both lied. You both betrayed people who trusted you. And now you're sitting here trying to make it sound like some tragic love story instead of the selfish reality a cruel betrayal."

Jada set down her cup. "I didn't ask you here to fight."

"Then why did you ask me here?"

She leaned back, crossed her legs. "Because I'm pregnant."

The air went out of me. I sat there with my mouth closed, throat tight, my tongue felt heavy.

"Three months," she said. Just letting it hang there. "Sebastian is the father. And before you ask, yes, Derek knows. He's already filing for divorce."

I picked up a sugar packet and turned it over and over in my fingers while I counted back. Three months. She'd conceived right around the same time Sebastian, and I had our last real conversation about trying for a baby the same night he'd told me, with such practiced sincerity, that he wanted to wait.

"Does Sebastian know?" My voice sounded like it belonged to someone else.

"He suspects." Her eyes held mine. "I wanted to tell you first.

Woman to woman."

"Woman to woman?" I laughed, harsh enough to make her flinch. "You don't get to play that card. You don't get to act like we're in this together."

"We are in this together, whether you like it or not." Her voice got aggressive like she had a right. "Sebastian is going to be the father of my child. This baby is not going away. And I think it's better for everyone if you just... let him go. File for divorce.

Move on. Stop dragging this out."

"Stop dragging this out... bitch?" I stood up, my chair scraping loudly against the floor. "I'm not the one who's been lying for months. I'm not the one who destroyed two marriages. You don't get to tell me what to do." I wanted to swing on her, pregnant and all.

Jada stood too, a crack forming in that composure. "I'm trying to be reasonable here, Eve. I'm trying to give you an out. But if you want to make this ugly, we can make it ugly."

"Is that a threat?"

"It's a reality check." She stepped closer, dropped her voice to a whisper. "Sebastian doesn't love you. He never did. You were convenient. Safe. The kind of woman his parents would approve of.

But you were never what he wanted."

It should have hurt more than it did. Standing there looking at this woman who'd helped take apart my marriage, I felt something I hadn't expected.

Clarity.

"You're right." Just a breath between us. "He probably never loved me. Not the way I deserved to be loved. But you know what? That says more about him than it does about me."

I grabbed my purse and walked out, leaving her standing there.

Three blocks. That's how far I got before I had to stop and lean against a building, hands shaking. Three months along with Sebastian's baby.

My phone rang; it was Sebastian.

I almost let it go. But something, anger, the need to look at him when I said what I had to say—made me pick up.

"Eve, we need to talk. Can I come over?"

"No." My voice was ice. "But I'm coming to you. Stay where you are."

I hung up.

He was at a hotel in Midtown, the kind of place that smells like new carpet and nothing. When he opened the door, he looked surprised.

"Eve, I didn't think"

"I just had coffee with Jada." I pushed past him. "Or should I say, I just got ambushed by your pregnant mistress."

His face went pale. "She told you."

"Oh, she told me a lot of things." I spun to face him. "She told me about your history. About how your parents forced you to end things.

About how I was just a convenient placeholder while you figured out how to get back to her."

"Eve, it's not..."

"Don't." I raised my hand. "Don't you dare tell me it's not what it sounds like. I'm done with the gaslighting. I'm done with the lies."

He ran a hand over his Caesar; I imagined the feeling of his waves were some kind of self-soothing mechanism for him. I used to find that endearing. Now I saw it for what it was—a stall.

He exhaled. "Okay. Okay. You want the truth? Here it is. Yes,

Jada and I have history. Yes, my parents made me end things with her. And yes, when I met you, I thought... I thought I could make it work. I thought I could be the man my parents wanted me to be."

"And now?"

"Now I don't know what I want." He looked at me, and I saw something real in his eyes—actual confusion. "I care about you, Eve. I do. But Jada... she's carrying my child. That changes everything."

"It changes everything." I let the syllables sit. "So, what was the plan, Sebastian? Were you going to tell me? Or were you just going to keep stringing me along while you played house with her?"

"I was trying to figure it out!" His voice broke open. "I was trying to do the right thing for everyone."

"The right thing?" I couldn't help but let out a grunt. "The right thing would have been not cheating on your wife. The right thing would have been being honest from the start. But you don't know how to do that, do you? You just know how to control. How to manipulate.

How to make everyone around you bend to what you want."

"That's not fair."

"Fair?" I stepped closer. "You married me knowing you were still in love with someone else. You made me feel crazy for questioning you. You gaslit me every time I asked about Jada. And now you're standing here acting like you're the victim in all this?"

His expression shifted. The confusion drained away, replaced by something colder. "You're not exactly innocent in this, Eve. You've been fucking Camden for a long damn time. Don't act like you're some saint."

"I started seeing Cam after I found out about you and Jada." The words came out clean and easy a lie I'd curated down to its bones. The truth—that my thing with Cam had started months before my encounter with Jada at his office—stayed submerged. I needed to be the wronged wife. I needed that story. It was the only version I could sleep inside of.

"After months of you making me feel like I was losing my mind. After you'd already checked out of this marriage."

"So that makes it okay?"

I stopped. The lie wanted to keep going, wanted to build me into the victim I needed to be. But something in his eyes—that cold calculation, his certainty we were the same—made me put it down.

"No." The word surprised even me, quiet and heavy between us. "It doesn't make it okay. I knew what I was doing. I was already with Cam when I suspected you had someone else." Admitting that was bitter on my tongue, like confessing to something I'd spent months convincing myself wasn't true. "But if I said that out loud... if I admitted that..."

I couldn't finish. Because if I admitted that, I'd have to look at what I'd actually become—someone just as willing to lie and cheat as he was. Someone who'd been rewriting history to stay comfortable inside her own story.

"At least I'm not pretending anymore." My voice was steady. "At least I'm not lying about what this is."

We stood there. I could see him recalibrating—when confrontation fails, Sebastian switches tactics. That was his pattern.

"Eve." His voice was softer now. He stepped toward me, reaching for my hand. "I know I've hurt you. I know I've made mistakes. But we can fix this. We can go to counseling. We can—"

I pulled my hand back. "Stop."

"Stop what?"

"Stop trying to manipulate me. Stop trying to make me believe that this is salvageable. It's not."

"You don't mean that." His hand moved toward my waist. "We have history. We have a life together. You can't just throw that away."

"Watch me." I stepped back. "I'm filing for divorce as soon as I can,

Sebastian. And I'm not changing my mind."

His expression went dark. "You're making a mistake."

"The only mistake I made was marrying you in the first place."

Something in him snapped—I saw it happen. The mask he had been wearing, that "let's make it work act" dropped all the way. "You think you can just walk away? You think you can humiliate me like this?"

"Humiliate you?" I stared at him. "This isn't about you."

"Everything is about me!" He grabbed my arm, hard. "I built this life. I gave you everything. And this is how you repay me?"

"Let go of me." I tried to steady my voice. My pulse was hammering.

"Or what?" His breath was hot on my face. "You'll run to

Camden? You'll play the victim? Everyone will see you for what you are—a gold digger who married up and couldn't handle it when things got real."

I looked at his hand on my arm. Then at his face. "If you don't let go of me right now, I'm calling the police."

For a moment, I wasn't sure what he was going to do next. Then he released me and stepped back, hands up.

"Get out." He demanded.

"Gladly."

My legs were shaking by the time I reached the elevator. I pressed the button and waited.

He poked his head out of the door and yelled. "You're going to regret this, Eve. When you're alone and broke and realize what you gave up—you're going to regret this."

I turned and looked at him one last time. "The only thing I regret is not leaving sooner."

The elevator doors closed. And then the tears came—not the quiet sad kind, but hot and stinging and pure rage. At Sebastian. At Jada. At myself for not seeing it sooner.

But underneath the rage was something else. Something that felt like relief.

I texted Cam: Can I come over? I need to see you.

He responded before I could put my phone down: Always. I'm here.

The elevator mirrors showed me my smudged makeup, my wrecked hair. Like I'd been through something.

Maybe I had, but I was still standing.

I knew what I wanted. Not what Sebastian needed, not what looked good on paper. I wanted out. I wanted to be loved by someone who really chose me, not as a placeholder, not out of convenience but as a real choice.

Cam.

The doors opened and I walked out into the lobby. The doorman nodded. I nodded back and stepped into the afternoon.

My phone buzzed. Sebastian: I'm sorry. Please don't do this. We can work it out.

I deleted it without responding thinking, this man must be crazy. He was ready to beat my ass just a few minutes ago.

There was nothing left to work out. The marriage had been over long before I'd let myself admit it.

In the cab on the way to Cam's, I heard Jada's voice again:

Sebastian doesn't love you. He never did.

And sitting in the back of the cab, watching the city, I realized something I hadn't expected. It didn't matter whether he'd loved me.

What mattered was that I was done letting that be the question.

The cab drove down the FDR drive, and I looked back at the skyline feeling some relief.

Goodbye, Sebastian. Goodbye to whoever I was when I was with you.

Hello to whatever comes next.

Chapter 11

THE FIVE MILLION DOLLAR SHADOW

With Sebastian gone, the high-rise finally felt like it had let some air in. Two thousand square feet stopped feeling like a holding cell. I stood at the edge of the sunken living room—the divorce decision still looming, but the dread had loosened. I could breathe.

I ran myself a bath. My phone dinged. Cam's text made me smile—we'd locked in plans to shop paint and furniture for my new place. When I saw him last, he casually mentioned that things with him and Tia had fizzled out and that they decided to just be friends.

I sank into the water and let myself imagine colored walls, a new start. But then Sebastian came back in. A memory from many nights ago: him in the steam-filled doorway, silent, watching the water rise. Not looking at me—just watching the depth of the tub with this flat, clinical stillness that had made every hair on my arms stand up.

I thought about what I was leaving. The California king bed

that was never a sanctuary. I rarely wore my designer clothes anymore. The walk-in closets, the modern bathroom, all of it. I'd traded what should've mattered for a tax bracket. I couldn't pretend I didn't know that anymore.

I scrubbed myself clean, let the water drain, and felt something else drain with it.

I took my coffee to the balcony in the morning and watched the light come up over the George Washington Bridge while the bridge hummed with early traffic. The other day Sebastian had stood on this same balcony, his eyes fixed on the drop to the pavement, moving in silence while he packed his bag. Folding each shirt like it was inventory. Talking about my "mental breakdown" like he was auditing a failing investment. When he finally looked at me, there was nothing there—just the measuring gaze of a man doing the math. Should I fight him for the apartment? I'd already run the numbers. This place would eat my savings before I could rebuild it. And the idea of bringing Cam here into rooms where Sebastian had controlled every inch of air—that felt wrong on all levels.

I needed to look at the lease. But more than that, I needed to confirm the shortfall I'd been suspecting. An investment banker doesn't turn her brain off when she walks in the door, and the math of our lifestyle hasn't been balancing for months. Sebastian kept his finances like a proprietary trade secret, but I'd flagged the discrepancies in our joint filings weeks ago. Time to find what he'd been hiding.

I went into his office with the same cold focus I'd use on a client's books. Sebastian hated me touching his things, said I threw off his vibe—but the data doesn't care about vibes. Behind the lease was a folder marked Confidential. Inside: bank notices confirming the shortfall I'd been running in my head. Numbers in the red. Stapled to them was my life insurance policy, the one I'd had for years, but recently, drastically amended. Five million dollars a new rider. Sebastian's name as sole beneficiary. My signature at the bottom, in my own hand.

I remembered those pages. He'd called them routine corporate filings for Whitmore & Robles. Slid them across the table and pointed to where I should sign. I'd been so exhausted by the marriage that I'd just signed, even though the banker in me had clocked the jump in premiums. This wasn't Sebastian being financially cautious. This was a hedge. A bet placed on my absence.

I called Grandma Locust to tell her movers would be bringing some of my things to the brownstone within the week. Then I thought about Kiki. I decided to show up the way she used to show up on me in college unannounced. Lance would be at work, Ethan at school. I grabbed two coffees and drove over.

Her cul-de-sac was a quiet loop of manicured lawns. Kiki had slid into this world seamlessly—entertainment executives, record label people, musicians for neighbors. Lance, an entertainment attorney, fit right in. The whole home division ran on BBQs and group vacations and proximity to semi-fame. Some of the wives had done a reality show. Kiki appeared a few times but wouldn't let herself get boxed in. The producers wanted drama. She was too grounded for their narrative.

I rang the doorbell. Her voice cut through the door before I even finished pressing it, she'd spotted me on the security system. She swung open the door in a pink yoga set with a matching sweatband.

"To what do I owe the pleasure?" she exclaimed, embracing me warmly. Spotting the coffee, she seized it with delight. "And you brought java? Okay, today must be my day!" She stepped aside to usher me in.

"I was off today and wanted to talk to you," I explained,

entering their home. The foyer had a large family portrait—Lance and five-year-old Ethan in tuxedos at a piano, both looking at Kiki draped across the baby grand in an elegant gold gown. Her confidence came off the canvas. Above, a skylight poured natural light down over everything.

I followed her through the kitchen to the sunroom. I took a bench by the floor-to-ceiling windows, letting the sun do its work.

Earth-toned pillows on the floor, lavender in the air.

"You know you're always welcome. Let me turn off my meditation music. I was just about to meditate and do some yoga," Kiki mentioned, preparing the space.

She pressed a remote and the soothing voice from the invisible speakers cut out. She took a sip of the coffee and her eyes closed. I'd added vanilla syrup—a small indulgence she wouldn't allow herself.

Her eyes shot open. "Wait, please tell me you have my dish in the car."

I gave her an apologetic look. "Sorry, Kiki, I totally forgot."

"Don't worry; I'll stop by your place later this week. But please have it out so I don't have to look for it."

"Your plate will be waiting," I assured her, rolling my eyes. "I came by because I wanted to tell you something."

"You're pregnant, aren't you? I knew it!" Kiki squealed.

"No, Kiki. Sebastian and I have decided to separate."

The bewilderment on her face was instant. She took another sip and sat across from me, taking my free hand.

"How could this have happened? What went wrong? You guys seemed so happy. Please don't tell me you're leaving him because of another woman. That's no reason to separate. Lance had this little thing with some young paralegal at the office. I saw inappropriate texts and pictures on his phone."

I gasped. Lance wasn't built like that, at least from what I could tell he was devoted to Kiki. Her face went hard and distant, like she was right back in that moment.

"Don't look so surprised. Lance isn't perfect! I reached out to that girl and told her to find some rapper's dick to suck, but to stay away from my husband because if she didn't, I'd skip the PTA meeting, lace up my sneakers, and drive straight from soccer practice to that fancy firm to beat her ass. I guess Lance told her I wasn't right in the head, so she stopped texting. At least, that's what it seems like. As for Lance, let's just say he won't be trying that again, or he'll get smarter about it. I had to meditate several times a day after that incident just to get back to myself. My energy healer did some reiki that cleared all that negative energy. It took me to a dark place." Kiki stood with her hands on her hips, lost somewhere in the memory, then snapped back. I took my opportunity to break her train of thought.

"I'm sorry you didn't feel like you could share that with me when you were going through it. I know we haven't been as close as we should be."

"And why is that? We used to be tight, Eve. Then you just... vanished, it feels like you've been avoiding me. What happened?" Kiki pouted.

"I wasn't avoiding you. I just didn't know how to fit into your new world, and the new friends you hang out with. I was scared of being judged, I guess. Things with Sebastian were worse than I let on—he was cruel, Keeks. A deviant. I started taking pills just to cope."

Kiki huffed loudly.

"I'm over all that now, including the pill-popping. It's been a lot,

Kiki, but things are looking up."

Kiki's eyes went wide before she spoke.

"Judgmental? Is that really how you see me? Eve, we're sisters. If you were using pills, you should have told me. I don't care who I'm hanging out with, we're family. I'm just pissed you went through that alone because you didn't think you could talk to me anymore. That doesn't fly."

Kiki sat next to me and covered my hand with hers.

"You don't have to fit in with them, Evie. It's always been us—you, me, and Grandma. I'm just in my feelings because you shut me out." "You're right, and for that, I have to apologize."

Kiki rolled her eyes and shook her head.

"So, you've stopped the pills, right? "You and Sebastian, what happened there?"

"No more pills," I said. And then the room tipped. A wave of vertigo, sudden and sickening, pulled the floor sideways. Kiki's face went pale and featureless at the center of my vision. I grabbed the edge of the bench, the rough fabric of the pillows grounding me. "Eve? You, okay? You look gray," Kiki said, her hand reaching for mine. "Just a head rush. Quitting the meds has me on edge," I managed, the room slowly leveling out. But as the nausea faded, something colder took its place. The amended policy. The five million. The bank notices and the shortfall. And Sebastian hovering lately, watching me with the same flat clinical focus he'd used on the bathtub. Fear moved down my spine, quiet and specific.

"As Grandma would say, Sebastian and I weren't equally yoked. Remember on my wedding day when you were helping me get dressed? You asked me if he was the one for me. You asked if I was sure I was marrying the man of my dreams."

"I remember. He was so different from the guys you usually dated. Quirky and uncool. He seemed to adore you possessively. But you seemed happy—or seemed to be. Your smile didn't reach your eyes like it did when you were with Camden. But you said you were happy, and every time I saw you, you acted like all was good."

"I thought I was. I was being shallow and materialistic. I was happy with all the material things I gained from our relationship. How silly of me! He was always generous with money and vacations. But Sebastian was critical of me in every way and emotionally abusive and a sexual mess. I can't believe I said that out loud, but he was. I wasn't the best wife; I stepped out of my marriage to feel like I controlled some part of myself and to get off." I laughed to stop myself from crying. It felt good to say this to Kiki.

"I didn't know he was emotionally unavailable. That's too much, Eve. I still can't believe you kept all this from me. Are you serious? To get off! Shit, he wasn't pleasing you, and he was emotionally abusive? Girl, why'd you stay married so long? You should've left; you didn't need to subject yourself to that. I'm scared to ask what you mean by saying he was a sexual deviant, but I guess that's for another time! I can't understand how you stayed these last few years if you weren't happy. You know we know plenty of attorneys you could've hired for a divorce!"

"I know. I just thought you work through it and make the best of it, doing whatever you must do along the way, including seeking physical pleasure and emotional stimulation by any means necessary. But we're way past that. I shouldn't have ever cheated on Sebastian. It wasn't right; despite his harsh ways, it's not the right thing to do, and I know better."

"It may not have been right, but if it was so bad that you had to seek outside men and drugs to get through, then he should be lucky that all you did was cheat. Do you think he cheated on you?"

"Oh, I know he cheated, Kiki. Her name is Jada — Jada Jennings. Same hometown as Sebastian, Bowie, Maryland. They go way back. She actually texted my phone and had the nerve to ask me to meet her at a Starbucks. I sat right across from her. She's married too — to a man named Derek — so we're both sitting here looking like fools on opposite sides of the same man. At this point she's the least of my concerns. I have a confession to make. I was waiting for you to ask who I cheated with, but since you haven't yet, I have to tell you. I circled back to a past relationship, and it didn't start off in the right way, but it's so familiar and comforting."

Kiki's eyes went wide. "You're back with Camden? The love of your fucking life! The one you should've married in the first place!" "Yes. My Cam, girl!" I gushed.

"Well, damn, we follow each other on the book and IG. He still looks good as hell, damn even better than he did growing up." Kiki blushed.

"Let me find out you be looking," I smirked and playfully elbowed her.

"I'm married, not blind, sis." Kiki smiled awkwardly. "Let me ask you a question: Why didn't you turn to God and pray or spirituality instead of turning to another man and pills when things got rough in your marriage? You could've talked to me or Grandma, but you chose not to."

"That's a good question; one I don't have the answer to. But when you know better, you do better, and that's just what I will do. Be better. Funny enough, Sebastian and I have come to a good place with this separation. At first he was upset but now he seems to be handling it well."

"I'm happy to hear that, but I'm still in shock. I wish I had been there for you more. You must emotionally prepare yourself for this. Even with all of his depravity, you've been with him for a few years. You go to sleep and wake up with him. It will take some time to adjust to the new norm. Not to mention, the emotional toll this can take. There's nothing worse than a messy divorce." Kiki looked at me with sadness in her eyes.

"I think I'm as prepared as I can be. Like I said, Sebastian knows it's not working; he doesn't want to rush to a divorce, though, so I will take my time with that part. There's no need to rush."

Kiki smiled deviously. "Anyway, sister, spill the beans. Tell me more about you and Cam!"

"Well, yeah, I'm talking to him and well yes, more than just talking. Rebuilding on what we had years ago. It's different now being with him as a grown-ass woman. He's different than he was at eighteen—improved in every way. He's got a good head on his shoulders despite the wrong turn he took when we were younger. He's a sweetheart and makes love to me in a way that feels so supernatural.

I feel whole when I'm with him. Not just in a sexual way. He listens to me; he's tender with me. We enjoy each other and laugh all the time when we're together." I gushed.

Kiki's face looked serious as she took it all in. "I understand all of that and I'm happy for you. Just take your time. Don't rush into this with Cam, or it'll be a rebound kind of thing and that won't be good for either of you. I do know that there's no feeling like being truly loved, and I'm happy for you. You deserve that.

So, what's next? Are you going to move, or is Sebastian?"

"I'm moving back home to Brooklyn—taking the ground-level apartment. And I quit my job." The words came out simple, but they landed like something seismic. Kiki's eyes widened. "I've been doing everything I thought I should do, and none of what I wanted to do. That apartment is my blank canvas—a space to figure out who I actually am."

The afternoon light shifted through the sunroom windows. Sitting there with Kiki—no pomp and circumstance, no explaining myself, no bracing for the next thing—I felt what I'd been missing. This was it.

Real. I could just be.

Back at the apartment, I texted Justin and Bella and told them everything that had happened with Sebastian and we promised to link up soon so that I could fill them in. It was one of the last nights I'd spend in the place Sebastian and I had called home. I wanted to fill it with the right energy before I left.

That evening, Cam invited me to dinner at a new spot in Greenpoint. A real date. Symbolic in the specific way first things always are—my first step into the next chapter as an actual single woman.

I treated myself to a haircut and twist-out to get ready. Grandma always said cutting your hair is shedding old energy. After years of Sebastian's grip on everything about me, the scissors felt deliberate. I put on stylish jeans, a crisp white tank, black four-inch pumps—casual with an edge.

When I pulled up, Cam was already outside waiting. His eyes lit up the second I stepped out. "You look amazing, baby! I love your haircut and your red lips." He looked easy and sharp himself—white tee, fitted jeans, fresh white sneakers, a black blazer that made him look like he'd stepped out of something curated.

"Eve. What's on your mind?" Cam's voice broke through the silence, his eyes searching mine.

I wanted to tell him exactly how badly I wanted him—every part of him pulling me in, the desire a low current that never quite shut off. I held it back.

"Babe, I've been grappling with some heavy stuff lately," I began, my voice soft but weighed down with the burden of my thoughts. "I'm trying to sift through the wreckage of this marriage and some other stuff I put myself in. Do you feel me?"

"I hear you, baby," Cam responded, his tone gentle but his eyes flickering to the phone buzzing in the center console. "What does Grandma Locust think about your situation with Sebastian? I know my sister is happy we've been back in touch, but my mom's is skeptical. She sees the drama with you being married to Sebastian and thinks I'm inviting a fire into a house I just finished building. I've worked too hard to get my HVAC business steady to let it all get messy again."

"She's supportive of me," I replied, a hint of gratitude in my voice. "And she's glad I've chosen to step away from him. I missed your mom; it'll be nice to be back in her and your sister's life. They were always so good to me."

"It's like we're both trying to piece together what could've been," Cam mused, his gaze distant as he reflected on our shared past. "Exactly," I agreed, feeling a pang of nostalgia for the dreams we once shared. "You were my first love, Cam. We had plans and dreams, and then life threw us a curveball."

"If only things had gone down differently," Cam sighed, a hint of regret lacing his words. "If I hadn't made those mistakes that led me astray while you were away at college...I didn't have to get myself locked up."

"You were young, and things happened," I reassured him, my voice softening with understanding. "You've turned your life around for the better. I'm so proud of you, Cam. You know we would've been married by now. We would've built a life together; I'd like to believe that."

"But we can't dwell on the 'what ifs,' Eve," Cam replied, his tone serious. "We have to deal with where we are now."

"So, where does that leave us, Cam?" I asked, a hint of uncertainty creeping into my voice. "Are we still hanging onto the memories of what once was, or is there something more for us in the future? We've been messing around with me as a married woman. Are you ready to take on dating and relearning me as a single woman? There's a difference."

"Eve, you've always had a piece of my heart," Cam confessed, his gaze turning serious. "But I'm not eighteen anymore. I've got a crew to manage and a supplier in Queens currently trying to bankrupt my expansion. I'm willing to wait for you, to be there for you when you've healed, but I need to know you're moving toward me, not just away from him. I can't be a backup plan while I'm out here trying to make something of myself. You already know how I get down, Eve. If it's going to be me and you, then that's what it's going to be."

"It's just tough, Cam," I admitted, my voice wavering with emotion. "Knowing that we could've had it all if things had played out differently."

"I know, Eve," Cam agreed, reaching out to squeeze my hand. "But maybe our paths had to take a detour so we could find ourselves here again. I want to be that person for you, but you have to be ready for me, Eve. I'm not going anywhere yet, but my life doesn't stop just because your marriage did."

"I hope not, Cam," I whispered, a tear escaping my eye.

"Because even though our love story hit a snag, it's still a chapter of my life that

I hold dear."

"Mine too, Eve," Cam said softly, his gaze meeting mine with warmth and affection. "Mine too."

I kept it real with him. Told him I was feeling him and wanted to keep going. What we had was real, and I appreciated the way he was holding me down while I sorted through all of it.

“Eve,” he said. “I hear you. And I’m not judging you; I told you I wouldn’t when we first started dealing with each other on this level. But don’t think for a second it’s easy. Every time you leave, I sit with it. All of it. I’m not trying to rush you, but I’m human. We’ll take it one step at a time, yeah? Just know I’m here for you, no matter what.”

That hit somewhere I wasn't expecting. It wasn't just the romance—it was having someone actually in my corner. I nodded back. "Thanks, Cam. I appreciate you more than you know." The conversation wasn't just about us—it was about the ground rules. How we'd move together through the next messy stretch.

Despite everything still unresolved, I had a friend in him. Someone willing to wait while I found my footing. And for the first time in a long while—maybe everything was going to be okay.

We lucked into a parking spot behind my car when we got back to his building, which when you found parking in Brooklyn feels like divine intervention. Cam turned off the car, got out, and came around to open my door. The Sauvignon Blanc had done its work—I was warm and loose and wanted to lick whatever was left on his lips.

When Cam asked, "Are you coming up?" I said, "Yup." He smirked, took my hand, and we went up.

Inside, he pulled me close and we kissed—the taste of the after-dinner mint still there. When we caught our breath, he grabbed a slim remote off the kitchen counter and the bass from the surround sound system filled the room.

He held me close, and I let myself go into him. My head on his shoulder, all the night's emotions pressing up behind my eyes. A tear slipped out, then another, quiet in the low light.

Cam tilted my chin up with two fingers. He looked at me, wiped the tears with his thumb. The kind of look that doesn't need words.

"You know how I feel about you; I loved your ass even when it wasn't player for me, too. I tried not to fall for you again, Evie, but I did because I never stopped loving you. So, you take whatever time you need, not too much though," he said, letting out a small chuckle. "But take the time you need because when we are together, I need your head to be in this with me. I know I got your body, but I need your mind too if we're ever going to make real moves."

I nodded. Cam didn't wrap his words in anything unnecessary. He said what he meant, it was always simple and unguarded. It always felt real. That was new. That was something.

I took his thumb in my mouth and sucked the salt off my own tears, looking at him, hoping my eyes said everything I wasn't saying out loud.

Cam picked me up. I wrapped my legs around his waist, and he carried me to the bedroom. Che'Le Marie came through the speakers.

"He said he'll make me a mother.

But he says he will make me a wife first

He's a special kind of lover

He makes sure that I always come first."

She sang as Cam lifted my tank top over my head. He stepped back, took his shirt off, reached around my back, and unsnapped my lacy black bra. My nipples stood at attention, ready for his tongue and his touch.

I reached for his face, grabbed him close. I sucked his bottom lip, one of my favorite things to do. I went for his pants, unbuckled his belt, and undid his jeans. I pulled them down as he undid my jeans and slid them and my panties down together. I stepped out of them, and he kneeled in front of me. He placed his head on my belly, and I held his head, running my hands over the rippled pattern in his hair. He leaned into my groin like he needed me. I stood there naked, him with his head buried in my groin, sniffing me, taking my scent in like it was a substance he could get high off. When he seemingly got enough, he gently parted my legs with his hands and stuck his head between my legs. Pressure, moisture, and heat radiated from his tongue as he licked me from the opening of my vagina to the swollen mound of nerves. He applied fast flickering pressure on my most sensitive spot. I couldn't stand still.

I was standing over him, and he was kneeling under me, having dessert.

Cam lifted my right leg over his shoulder, giving him more access to my inner parts. I thought I would lose my balance. I was ecstatic as I grinded my pelvis against his mouth, ensuring he got every desired drop. When I quivered and shook from the eruption my body released, I nearly folded, weak from the orgasm I had just experienced. Cam rose, scooped me up, and laid me across his bed. I lay there, feeling more relaxed than I had in years. I closed my eyes, and when I opened them again, Cam handed me a glass of ice water. I sat up and took a few sips. He sipped from the same glass, watching me. I lay back against his soft comforter and sank in.

Cam reached down and massaged my head, running his thick fingers through my newly cropped curly mane. That massage was just what I needed; my own moisture seeped in between my thighs.

Cam grabbed an ice cube from the glass and lay down beside me. His sexy, crooked smile disappeared as he licked his lips. He took the ice and circled my nipple; I jerked involuntarily from the coolness and the sensation that traveled back down to my sweet spot. Cam covered my mouth with his and kissed me deeply. I wanted to swallow his tongue; it tasted so good.

He positioned himself over me, and I opened my legs to welcome him in. As Sade cooed, "If you were mine..." Cam's engorged third leg opened me and filled me up. I inhaled, taking him all in. I pulled him deeper, our breaths hitching in the same ragged rhythm. Deep moans and sighs escaped his lips as he pushed deeper inside me. His body moved, his stomach rippling as he worked. Like he was dancing to a slow reggae tune only he could hear. He held on to my hips to stop me from moving, trying to slow his eruption. I ignored his gesture and stroked my canal against his shaft until he pulled himself out of me and poured himself onto my belly. He panted, kissed me, and rolled over to lie next to me.

"Let me get a towel," he said as he attempted to get up.

"I'll get it. Relax, baby." I patted him on the arm and pointed to the bed.

I made my way to the bathroom. Looked at myself in the

mirror—hair all over my head.

I smiled. Finally free, desired, loved.

When I came back, Cam had poured us both glasses of orange juice, and there was a bottle of champagne with two flutes on the nightstand. He patted the bed, and I scampered over, giddy as a schoolgirl.

"Round two," Cam said, reaching for the remote and turning the music up. "I don't want anyone to hear you, but I'm okay if they do too."

I smirked as the familiar beat dropped.

Chapter 12

THE HACKER'S INHERITANCE

Three days later the apartment was shedding its skin. Boxes lined the hallway like sentinels guarding the exit of a life I didn't recognize anymore. The marble floors, once mirror-polished, were scuffed now, tracked with the grit of moving day. I walked through the sunken living room, my footsteps cracking off the white stone. It was still beautiful, but the beauty had curdled. Every surface was a reminder of what I'd traded for security — and what security had quietly become.

I kept going back to the office. Usually I avoided it — cold glass and brushed steel, permanently saturated with Sebastian's cologne and the smell of expensive electronics, the room where he ran our lives like a portfolio. But that life insurance notification I'd found days ago had turned it into a crime scene in my mind, and I couldn't leave it alone. I needed to know how deep I was already in.

I sat in his chair, leather cooling against the backs of my legs. Everything was too clean. The desk was nearly empty — just the monitor and a single silver pen. I'd given him that pen for our third anniversary. He never used it to write. He kept it positioned on the blotter with a precision that was almost ceremonial. I'd watched him through the doorway enough times to know he didn't pick it up, he aligned it — the clip matched to a microscopic notch in the desk's steel inlay. I mimicked the motion, and a port I'd always mistaken for a structural bolt vibrated once and released a slim, matte-black drive.

My heart turned over slowly. I stared at that drive the way you stare at a live coal someone's dropped at your feet. No note, no label — Sebastian didn't leave hints for people who weren't supposed to find things. But his logic was a map I'd spent five years memorizing. There was a sequence he'd made me commit to memory years ago, called it an emergency backup, called it Aegis. He thought I'd forgotten it the day we left the old apartment. I didn't. Those numbers were carved into me.

I needed Marcus. We'd worked together in mid-market investment years ago, back when I was still the kind of person whose life could be measured by spreadsheets. He was the one who'd fixed my coffee-destroyed laptop without a word, who knew how to move through digital systems like they owed him a favor. Information was his currency, and he spent it wisely.

The coffee shop in Jersey City was loud enough to be anonymous. Marcus sat across from me, face lit blue by a ruggedized laptop that looked like it had survived something worse than I had. He didn't comment on the fact that I was shaking. He just took the drive, plugged it in, and went to work.

"This is high-level encryption, Eve," he whispered, eyes on the screen. "Two-hundred-fifty-six-bit. But it's the signature on the partition that matters. Aegis. The FBI has been chasing this specific signature for years. This isn't just someone hiding his browsing history; it's a federal indictment waiting to happen."

"Can you get in?" I asked, my voice thin. I kept watching the door, half-expecting Sebastian to walk through it with that slow, knowing smirk — the one that meant he'd already won something I didn't know we were playing for.

"I don't need to crack it," Marcus said, as I recited the alphanumeric string I'd carried since the beginning. "You already had the keys. Aegis. It's a cloud-based dead man's switch. If he doesn't log in every forty-eight hours, the contents of this drive are supposed to be distributed to a list of pre-set recipients. But he's been diligent. The timer hasn't tripped."

He hit a key, and the screen opened up. I leaned in. The roasting coffee smell suddenly turned my stomach. These weren't tax returns. They were logs. Transmissions. Proprietary data from three of the biggest tech firms on the East Coast — hardware schematics that hadn't been released yet, IPO marketing strategies still in the quiet period, CEO dossiers that read like blackmail manuals.

"He's not an IT consultant, Eve," Marcus said, voice dropping to something jagged. "He's an interceptor. He's been selling this data to their rivals through a series of offshore shells. This is corporate espionage on a massive scale."

The floor tilted. Every piece of jewelry, every bottle of wine, every vacation — dividends from a criminal enterprise. The names of his clients were men whose faces were on magazine covers, men who didn't use lawyers to settle things.

"Look at this," Marcus said, clicking into a folder labeled Liquidation. "He's been draining the domestic accounts for months. Moving the money into a series of accounts in the Cayman Islands and the Seychelles. It's a systematic exit strategy."

There it was. The life insurance policy, a cold entry under the Capital Infusion tab. Beside it, a date circled in red. Weeks away.

My name was a line item. A projected revenue stream.

It clicked into place all at once. The five million wasn't about Jada. It wasn't about a bitter divorce or a fresh start. The feds were closing in, and Sebastian needed one last liquidity event before he disappeared entirely. I was the collateral. The final payout.

"Eve? You're white as a sheet," Marcus said, reaching for my arm. "We need to take this to the authorities. This isn't just a cheating husband. This is dangerous."

"I can't just go to the local precinct," I whispered, the word tasting like copper. "I need this to be the centerpiece of his trial, not just a backup plan. Attempted murder is a state charge — he could buy a high-priced defense or vanish on bail. But if I involve the FBI now, they'll be in that courtroom with a federal indictment that no amount of money can move. It's the only way to ensure he stays buried for good."

I kept seeing the way he'd looked at me in the tub. Not at his wife. At an investment approaching maturity. He was waiting for the optimal moment, solving for the only variable left — my pulse.

"Give me the drive," I said, with my hand out. "And the credentials. Everything."

"Eve, don't be stupid. You can't go back there," Marcus said.

"People like this, they don't just let you walk away with the ledger."

"I'm already gone, Marcus. I just need to make sure I stay that way."

I walked out into the evening. The city looked different now — the skyline lit up like a thousand eyes, every black sedan a potential threat, every man in a tailored suit a possible associate of the man I'd been sleeping next to for five years. The apartment wasn't a home. It was a trap with good lighting, and the predator was already inside, watching the clock.

I hailed a cab and sat rigidly during the whole ride; fingers cramped around the drive in my pocket. My reflection in the window was a ghost — wild curls framed by passing streetlamps, a woman on the edge of something. But the fog I'd been living in for months felt thinner now, burned off by the cold clarity of what I knew. The pills, the policy, the Aegis files — all of it spelling out the same thing. My death, scheduled and budgeted.

I wasn't just a wife or a mistress or a victim. I was the only person who knew the truth, and in Sebastian's world, that made me the most dangerous asset he had.

When the cab pulled up to our building and the darkened penthouse windows loomed above me, I didn't look away. This wasn't a domestic dispute anymore. It was a war. And I finally knew the rules.

I got out of the car, the drive cold against my thigh. I had a digital bomb in my pocket — the kind that could turn a murder attempt into a federal espionage case. The question wasn't whether I could survive him. It was whether I could survive the fallout when I handed the FBI the keys to his kingdom.

Chapter 13

THE POISONED GIFT

The coffee was already brewing when I finally dragged myself out of bed, steam curling thin in the morning light. I'd mapped this day for weeks, the liberation, the clean exit — but the 6:00 a.m. alarm hung over the apartment like something I couldn't name. I texted Sebastian to confirm he'd wait until I was gone before coming back. He said he would.

I packed everything except Kiki's dish on the counter; I planned to stop by her place and drop it off before I left for Brooklyn.

The apartment stretched out across two thousand square feet — sun through the kitchen, the sunken living room, the balcony, the quiet rear wing where we'd slept. I lit incense and put on a playlist. Keyshia Cole filled the rooms: "If he ain't gonna treat you the way he should, just let him goooo." I danced and cleaned, moving room to room, making sure the place was spic and span the way Sebastian liked it. But I couldn't stop thinking about him two nights ago in the bathroom doorway, staring at the garden tub with something flat in his eyes. He'd been muttering about declining investments, obsessing over a folder marked "confidential". I'd written it off as his usual control thing. But the way he'd looked at the water, eyes narrow and gone somewhere else, had stayed with me.

The sound of the doorbell rang, breaking me out of my thoughts. Tom and the movers arrived and loaded everything onto dollies. I tipped them, closed the door, and leaned against it. The apartment had gone hollow.

Then there was a loud knock, I assumed it was the movers coming back to double check that they hadn't forgotten anything. I opened it to a young delivery guy with a gift basket. "Delivery for Mrs. Eve Whitmore," he said.

I reached for my wallet, but he waved me off — "already tipped" — and left with a smile. I carried the basket to the marble island and pulled the card. Bash's handwriting: "A toast to your new life. I wish you nothing but the best, Eve. With love, Bash."

Gardenias. My favorite red wine. Chocolates, fruit, cheese, crackers. I cranked up the music and danced while I ate, pouring glass after glass of that sweet red.

By evening I'd ordered pasta and finished the wine in the fridge. I was drowsy in a way that felt heavy, heavier than it should have, but I lit the candles in the tiled alcove anyway, laid out my robe and warm towels, added magnesium and lemongrass oil to the bath, part of my usual ritual. My one reliable thing. I dropped my clothes and sank into the water, settled back against the bath pillow, closed my eyes.

I was sleepier than I should have been. I told myself I'd get out soon. My eyes wouldn't stay open. The music cut off.

Paralysis dropped onto me like a stone. I fought to lift an arm, a finger — nothing. The panic was sharp and immediate, screaming through my mind while my body refused every command. I thought it was a dream until I heard Bash laugh — that low, clipped sound.

I couldn't make his words out over the roaring in my ears. I told my limbs to push up, to fight, but I had nothing. Then Sebastian's face above the rim, his lips brushing my forehead felt like little razor blades.

"You thought you were so slick, bitch," he said.

My mind was completely awake. Trapped, screaming, fully conscious behind a body that had stopped working. I tried to scream.

Nothing came out. He leaned down — satisfaction in his eyes, that clinical satisfaction — and kissed me again.

The water reached my nose. He leaned in again, face close, all malice and calm. My tears ran into the water. I couldn't even turn my head.

My vision started to blur. Sebastian's face, eyes wild and wide, and then he was gone. Pain exploded through my chest. I wanted it to stop. Faces flashed — Grandma, Kiki, my mother, Cam — everything I hadn't said. The darkness took him, and then it took everything.

My life stuttered past in fragments. Then a blast of bright gold light swallowed the room. I drifted upward, out of the body in the water, shedding it the way you shed a wet coat. From the ceiling I watched that girl, and the pain finally left. I turned toward the warmth. The world dissolved.

- ✧ -

Fate moved in the silence between floors. Sebastian rode elevator A down while Kiki came up in elevator B. She just wanted her plate. Her stubbornness kept me alive.

She burst into the apartment calling my name. Something — instinct, a chill she couldn't explain — she picked up her plate but something pulled her past the kitchen and down the hall. She found me under the water. The ceramic dish hit the tile in pieces as she lunged for the tub, screaming. She hauled me over the porcelain rim and slammed her palms into my chest. I choked water up but didn't wake. Kiki dialed 911 with one hand, sobbing the news to Grandma Locust with the other.

The ICU's mechanical pulse was the first thing to pierce the fog — a steady counting of the four days I'd lost. Doctors murmured nearby about oxygen levels and recovery windows, but my mind came back steady. When the sedation finally cleared, Grandma Locust was there, cheeks wet. Kiki sat by the wall, exhausted, still managing to look put-together. And Cam — leaning over me, his crooked smile, a long exhale of relief.

A nurse came to check my IV. Then Dr. Jonathan Williams — I recognized him from somewhere, weeks back — walked in with a measured stride. He laid out what had happened: Kiki's intervention had been the margin, and when I'd arrived, there was a serious amount of Valium and ketamine in my system. He was relieved to see me awake. He also needed to understand the drugs.

The staff assumed I'd done it to myself. Grandma Locust, Kiki, and Cam pushed back on that, hard. Despite the separation, they'd tried to reach Sebastian. He didn't answer. He was still my husband of five years, and they expected at least that much — some acknowledgment that I was in the ICU, that I had almost died.

My throat was raw from the breathing tube. Every attempt to speak came out like a scrape of sandpaper. But there was something I had to get out.

Grandma Locust handed me a pen and pad. She knew me.

I wrote Sebastian's name. She stared at it. Kiki opened her mouth, some reflex to explain it away — and I shook my head, sharp, once.

"Sebastian did this." The words came out in a scratchy whisper, but they landed. I watched Grandma Locust's face move through shock and then darken into something harder and older.

The room went still.

"Kiki, call the police. Now!" Grandma Locust's voice left no room.

Kiki had her phone out before the sentence finished. I whispered to Grandma what I could — the ghost of a kiss on my forehead, the paralysis, the sound of his voice.

Sebastian had miscalculated. He'd assumed Kiki wouldn't find me in time. He'd left the country with two tickets to Paris, coming back when he probably thought he was clear — until he heard her voicemails about my condition.

He'd been organizing offshore accounts, preparing a new life. The police pulled him from his office late that night; he'd gone back to retrieve files on a thumb drive. One last arrogant move. In hindsight, he should have sent Jada. She was barely four months along, her stomach just beginning to show, and it seems she'd always been the more careful one.

Chapter 14

THE FIRST STEP

The waiting room at "Our Minds Matter" smelled like lavender and something else I couldn't place — sandalwood, maybe. Cedar. It was supposed to be calming. My hands still wouldn't stop trembling as I filled out the intake forms. Name. Date of birth. Emergency contact.

Then the section asked why I was seeking therapy.

Where do I even begin?

My pen clicked against the clipboard — a nervous tic I'd picked up somewhere. My husband tried to kill me. I was having an affair. I use sex and substances to cope with feelings I can't name. My mother died when I was young, my father walked out before I was born. I feel empty most of the time, even surrounded by people who love me.

I wrote: "Recent trauma. Preparing for upcoming legal testimony.

Difficulty coping with the pressure."

It felt like describing the ocean by mentioning it was wet.

"Evelyn?" A woman's voice from the doorway. She stood still, watching me with a calmness that made my breath catch. She didn't look like a doctor. She looked like a woman who already knew which secrets I was keeping.

"It's Eve," I said, smoothing my jeans as I stood. I'd changed three times that morning, I settled on casual. I didn't want to look like I was trying too hard, but I also didn't want to look like I was coming apart.

Even though I was.

"Eve," she said, warm. "I'm Dr. Amara Chen. It's nice to meet you.

Come on back."

Her office was smaller than I expected, but it felt lived-in. A big window over a small garden. Two comfortable chairs facing each other, a side table between them with a tissue box, a small plant, and a sound machine running white noise. Abstract art down the hallway — swirls of blue and green that reminded me of water.

I sat. She picked up a leather-bound notebook. "So, Eve, what brings you here today?"

The question sat in the air. I'd rehearsed this. But now the words were stuck in my throat like cotton.

"I..." I started, then stopped. My eyes burned. "I don't even know where to start."

"That's okay." Her voice was a soft landing. "There's no right or wrong place to begin. Why don't you tell me what's been happening recently? What made you decide to reach out?"

I gripped the arms of the chair. "My husband tried to kill me last month. He drugged me and tried to make it look like an accident for the insurance money. Now the trial is only weeks away, and the prosecutor says my testimony is the lynchpin of the whole case. But every time I think about seeing him in that courtroom, I stop being able to breathe."

She stayed neutral, but something moved across her face — concern, or maybe just recognition. She nodded slowly. "That is a shattering experience, and the weight of a trial only adds to that burden. I'm so sorry you're carrying all of this. How are you feeling right now, at this moment?"

"Numb," I said. "Most of the time, just numb. And then sometimes, out of nowhere, I feel everything all at once, and it's too much. My chest gets tight. I feel like I'm drowning."

"Those sound like panic attacks," Dr. Chen said, making a note.

"Have you experienced those before, or is this new since the incident?"

"I've had moments before where I felt overwhelmed, but nothing like this. These are... different. Worse."

"Trauma can manifest in many ways," she said. "Our bodies hold onto experiences even when our minds try to move past them. But Eve, I want you to know that what you're feeling is a normal response to an abnormal situation. You're not broken."

The tears came. "I don't feel normal. I feel like I'm losing my mind. And the worst part is..." I paused, the shame landing heavy. "The worst part is that I wasn't even faithful to him. I was having an affair with my ex-boyfriend. So maybe I deserved—"

"Stop right there." Dr. Chen's voice was a steady anchor. "Nothing you did—no choice you made, no affair, nothing—justifies someone trying to take your life. Do you understand that? Whatever happened in your marriage, whatever choices you made, you did not deserve to be murdered."

I nodded. I didn't fully believe it.

"Tell me about the affair," she said. "Not because I'm judging you, but because I want to understand what was happening in your life before the incident."

I wiped my face with the back of my hand. She pushed the tissue box closer. I took one and held it.

"The worst part is..." I stopped. "The worst part is that I told Sebastian I only started seeing Cam after I found out about his mistress. That's not true. I was already with Cam when I started suspecting something was wrong. I was already lying in our marriage before he ever lied to me. I told myself it was because he checked out first, stopped paying attention — but..."

"But?" A quiet nudge.

"But I chose it anyway. I knew what I was doing. And when it all came out, I rewrote the story, so I'd be the victim and he'd be the villain. Now I'm not even sure what's true anymore."

Saying it out loud made it real. I'd spent months building a version of events where I was entirely wronged, entirely blameless. Sebastian's cruelty was real — that part didn't change — but the rot in our marriage had roots I'd watered. The affair wasn't just passion or loneliness. It was a choice I made a hundred small times before it became something I couldn't undo. Sitting in that chair under Dr. Chen's steady gaze was the first time I let myself be guilty of something and still worth saving. Both things are true at once.

I sat there, the tissue twisted in my fingers, my chest still tight from everything I'd just said.

Dr. Chen let the silence sit for a moment.

"When you think about Sebastian," she said, "what hurts the most?"

I swallowed. "That I didn't tell the truth. Not really. I twisted it.

Even to myself."

"And before everything came out?" she asked. "Before the affair... what was your relationship like?"

I hesitated. "Fine," I said, a little too fast. "Normal, I guess."

She gave a small nod, like she'd heard that answer a hundred times before. "'Fine' can mean a lot of things."

I exhaled, my shoulders dropping. "It was probably never fine. I thought he was utterly in love with me with his obsessive ways or maybe I just felt like he loved me. I don't know. Something shifted, and instead of dealing with it, I just... filled the space."

"With Cam."

I nodded.

"And what did Cam give you that felt missing?"

I stared down at my hands. "Attention. Desire. He made me feel... chosen. He knows me, the me before the degrees before the luxury high rise living. "

Saying it out loud made it sound smaller than it felt.

"Chosen," Dr. Chen repeated.

I shrugged. "I don't know. It sounds stupid."

"It doesn't," she said. "That matters more than people like to admit."

I didn't respond. Just sat there, picking at the edge of the tissue.

"And when you didn't feel chosen," she asked gently, "what did that feel like?"

I opened my mouth to answer... then stopped.

Because it wasn't just about Sebastian.

It felt older than that. Familiar in a way I couldn't quite explain. "I don't know," I said finally, quieter now. "Just... empty, I guess."

She nodded, not pushing.

"We can come back to that," she said.

I let out a small breath, not realizing I'd been holding it.

Because I knew there was more there.

I just wasn't ready to say it yet.

"This is all a very common response to trauma and grief," Dr. Chen said. "When we're in pain, we often look for ways to numb it or escape it. Sex, substances, even work — these can all become ways we avoid dealing with difficult emotions."

"Is that what I was doing with Cam? Avoiding my feelings about

Sebastian?"

"What do you think?"

I hated it when therapists did that. Turned it back around. But I sat with it.

"I think..." The words took effort. "I think being with Cam

made me feel like myself again. Like the person I was before, everything got so complicated. Sebastian was always watching, always questioning. With Cam, I could just... breathe. I could be messy and imperfect, and he didn't try to fix me."

"It sounds like Cam represented freedom to you," Dr. Chen said. "A return to a time before the losses, before the pain. But Eve, we can't go backward. We can only move forward."

My shoulders went up. "I know that. I'm not trying to go back to college or pretend I'm sixteen again."

"I don't think you are." She didn't blink. "But I do think you might be seeking something in Cam that you need to find within yourself first. The feeling of being whole of being enough just as you are — that can't come from another person, no matter how much we love them."

That landed like a fist to my stomach. Because somewhere underneath everything, I knew she was right. I'd been running this loop — Cam, some guys in between, then Sebastian, then Cam again.

Looking for someone to confirm that I was real, that I was worth it.

"I don't know how to be whole on my own," I whispered. "I don't even know who I am without someone else defining me."

"Then that's what we're going to work on," she said. "Getting to know Eve. Not Eve the daughter, or Eve the wife, or Eve the girlfriend. Just Eve."

"What if there's nothing there?" I know I sounded small and scared. "What if I look inside and find out I'm just... empty? How am I supposed to stand up in front of a jury and be a 'strong witness' if there's nothing left of me?"

"You're not empty, Eve. You're hurt. There's a difference." She leaned forward. "I want to try something with you. Close your eyes for a moment."

I hesitated, then did it.

"Take a deep breath in through your nose, hold it for four counts, then release it slowly. Good. Again."

My heart started to slow.

"Now think back to before all the pain, before the losses. Think of yourself as a little girl. What did you love to do? What made you happy?"

Pictures came. Me at seven or eight, dancing in the living room to my mother's old records — the feeling of music moving through my body, pure and free. Me at ten with a notebook, writing whole worlds where I was in charge and the endings were good. Me at twelve, in my grandmother's garden — the smell of earth, the satisfaction of watching something grow.

"I loved to dance," I said, eyes still closed. "And write. And garden with my grandmother. I loved creating things, making things grow." "When was the last time you did any of those things?"

I opened my eyes. The answer was right there on my face. Years.

"Life got in the way."

"Or maybe you got lost along the way." She didn't rush it. "Eve, trauma doesn't just affect us the moment it happens. It changes how we see ourselves, how we move through the world. Your father, leaving before you were born, taught you that you weren't worth staying for. Your mother's death taught you that love is temporary and painful. Cam and your initial break-up may have told you that you're not enough. And Sebastian — his control, his betrayal, what he did — told you that you can't trust your own judgment."

The tears ran while she mapped it. Each loss had carved away a piece of me until I was hollow, filling the space with whoever would tell me I was worth something, even briefly.

"But here's what I want you to understand," she said, steady and warm. "None of those things were about you. Your father's leaving was about him, his own inability to handle what life asked of him. Your mother's death was a tragedy, not a verdict. Cam was young and scared and didn't know how to hold your heart or perhaps you didn't know how to hold his. And Sebastian is a man with serious problems who made terrible choices. None of that is a statement about your worth. That includes the version of you who has to face him in court. You aren't testifying as a victim, Eve. You're testifying as the woman who survived him and is taking her story back."

"Then why does it feel like it is?" I asked through my tears. "Why do I feel like I'm unlovable to the core?"

"Because that's the story you've been telling yourself for so long that you've started to believe it's true. But stories can be rewritten. That's what we're going to do here — examine these beliefs, challenge them, build a new version. One where you're the author of your own life."

I grabbed another tissue. "I don't know if I can do that."

"You don't have to know right now. You just have to be willing to try. Can you do that?"

I let the silence sit before answering. Did I want to keep living this way — bouncing person to person, using whatever would numb the ache, never once at peace? Or was I ready to do the actual work, even if it meant facing every ugly thing I'd been running from?

"Yes. I can try."

"That's all I'm asking." She smiled. "Now. I want to give you some homework before our next session."

A dry laugh escaped me. Homework.

"Journal every day. It doesn't have to be long — even a few sentences. Write about your feelings, your thoughts, what happened. And do one thing each week that you loved as a child. Dance, write, garden — whatever calls to you. We need to reconnect you with the parts of yourself that got lost."

"Okay," I said, though the journaling made me uncomfortable. Writing meant being honest, and I'd spent so long lying to myself I wasn't sure I remembered how.

"And Eve?" she added as I stood to leave. "Be gentle with yourself. Healing isn't linear. There will be good days and bad days. The goal isn't perfection; it's progress."

I walked out through the lavender-scented waiting room carrying something I hadn't felt in a long time. Hope. Thin as paper. But there.

Maybe I wasn't done. Maybe, with enough time and work and honesty, I could find my way back — or better, find my way forward to the woman I was supposed to become.

I sat in my car, pulled out my phone, opened notes.

Day One, I typed. I went to therapy. I cried. I admitted things I've never said out loud. It was terrifying and exhausting and somehow... freeing. Dr. Chen says I'm not broken. I'm not sure I believe her yet, but I want to. God, I want to.

I saved it and started the car. The courthouse no longer felt like a place where I'd be taken apart. It felt like a place where I might finally speak.

A beginning. Small, imperfect, mine.

Chapter 15

PAPER TRAILS AND PICKET FENCES

The hospital was fluorescent purgatory. Air that had been scrubbed of everything useful, bleach smell underneath everything, the low hum of machines doing the work that bodies couldn't. Grandma Locust lay in the adjustable bed at the center of the room, her formidable frame looking strange against all that white — smaller than she ever looked anywhere else. A minor stroke, the doctors said, as if ruptures in the brain came in sizes that didn't count.

To me, the floor had shifted an inch to the left and everything I knew was slightly wrong.

Kiki sat in the plastic chair by the window, fingers flying across her phone. Even in a crisis, Kiki had her armor up — sleek ponytail, lint-free yoga pants, worry channeled into productivity. She was coordinating childcare, confirming dinner delivery for Lance, somehow managing not to look like she was unraveling. I envied her distraction. My own life was still a series of empty rooms and new prescriptions, a quiet apartment I was slowly learning to inhabit without the sound of Sebastian's footsteps.

"The neurologist said she should be home by Tuesday," Kiki whispered, still looking at her screen. "But she can't climb stairs yet. We need to move her bed to the parlor. And someone has to handle the tenants. You know how she is about the brownstones — she treats those rental agreements like sacred texts."

I watched Grandma Locust. Eyes closed, breathing heavy. She was the sun this family orbited around, the gravity that kept us from drifting into the ether. Seeing her still like that was a physical ache. "I'll do it," I said. My voice came out steadier than I felt. "I'll handle the archives. Manage the properties until she's back on her feet."

Kiki finally looked at me, something softening in her face for just a moment. "You sure, Eve? You've got enough on your plate with the recovery and the... well, everything."

"I need the work, Kiki. I need to be busy and not just in the house. It's better than sitting downstairs in my apartment counting the minutes until my next session with Dr. Chen."

The brownstone felt different when I got back that evening. It breathed — cedar, old lace, the ghost of Grandma's Sunday roasts. Without her, the silence had weight. I went to the parlor where the archives lived. A chaotic library of Brooklyn history: yellowed lease agreements, handwritten receipts from the seventies, folders overflowing with utility bills, all crammed into a massive oak desk and a row of mismatched filing cabinets.

I spent three days submerged in it. Managing her properties wasn't really about real estate — it was about people. Notes about a tenant's daughter's graduation. Reminders to drop the rent for the elderly man in 3B every winter. A map of a life built on service and survival, nothing like the transactional cold machine Sebastian had curated for us. My hands stayed stained with ink and dust. It felt honest.

Grounding.

On the fourth afternoon, I found the trunk. Back of the parlor closet, buried under heavy wool blankets that smelled of mothballs and decades. A steamer trunk, leather straps cracked, brass buckles gone dull gold. It was locked, but the key was where Grandma kept everything that mattered: in a small velvet pouch inside a hollowed-out book on the mantle. The lock clicked open like permission.

No property deeds. No tax returns. Layers of tissue paper protecting a life I only knew in pieces. A pair of baby shoes. A lock of hair tied with a blue ribbon. And at the bottom, a bundle of envelopes tied with fraying twine, addressed to me — stamps never canceled. Unsent. The return address on every one was the same: The Serenity Center for Women, Hudson Valley.

My mother's handwriting. Dominique's loops, rushing across each envelope like she couldn't get the words down fast enough. My heart knocked hard against my ribs.

I had spent twenty years believing I was an afterthought. That she loved her habit more than she loved me. I'd built my whole identity around that gap — looked for men like Sebastian to fill what she'd carved out. And here were letters she'd written and never sent.

I opened the first one. The paper thin as dried leaves. My Dearest Eve. The doctors say I have to write the things I can't say. They call it a bridge to the outside. But how do I build a bridge to a daughter who deserves a mother who isn't broken?

I read through the night. The lamp cast long shadows across the floorboards, and I didn't move. These weren't the ramblings of someone who forgot me. They were dispatched from a war. She wrote about the physical agony of early sobriety, the craving like fire in her marrow. She wrote about the guilt that kept her from calling — a shame so heavy she was afraid her voice would shatter me. She described her dreams for my future: she wanted me to dance, to see the world, to be a woman who never felt the need to hide.

I'm fighting my way back to you, Eve, she'd written in the final letter, dated months before she died. Every day I get clean is a day I earn the right to see your face again. Grandma says you're getting so tall. She says you have my eyes but your own spirit. Don't let the world dim it, baby. I'm coming home. I promise.

She never made it. Her last relapse had always felt like a final answer — I wasn't enough to keep her here. But sitting on that dusty parlor floor, surrounded by her words, I understood something different. She hadn't been running from me. She'd been trying to run toward me while her legs were weighted with lead. She wasn't a negligent ghost. She was a woman who had been drowning and using her last breath to say I love you.

I sat on that parlor floor until the room went dark around me. At some point I stopped reading and just held the bundle of letters against my chest. I hadn't prayed — really prayed, not the rote kind — since before the tub. Some part of me had decided, somewhere in the months of sedation and survival, that I didn't have the standing for it anymore. Too much had happened that I'd chosen. Too much mess of my own making.

But sitting there in Grandma Locust's parlor with my mother's handwriting on my lap, I started anyway. Not out loud. Not with the right words. Just the raw inside of me, turned upward, with nowhere else to go. Something like: I don't know if You've been watching all of this, but if You have, I need You to know I'm tired of being the person who holds it together. I'm tired of being strong. I don't even know who I am underneath it all. But I'm still here. And I don't think that's an accident. So, whatever You have left for me, I'm willing to try.

It wasn't church and it wasn't elegant. But it was the most honest thing I'd said in years. And afterward, the room felt different. I didn't feel fixed or healed, just less alone.

The tears came slowly — not the sharp, jagged sobs of the tub, but something warmer. The sound of a fence coming down. A barrier I'd built to protect myself from a history I'd misread. I wasn't a girl who had been abandoned. I was a girl who had been loved by a woman who simply didn't have the strength to survive her own storms.

Two days later I was back in Dr. Chen's office, the bundle of letters in my lap. Afternoon sun through the blinds in clean gold strips. She didn't offer a tissue or a platitude. She waited.

"I've been living in a story that wasn't true," I said, voice barely there. I traced the looping D on the top envelope. "I thought the reason I stayed with Sebastian, the reason I let him control me, was because I was trying to prove I was worth keeping. I thought if I was perfect enough, no one would leave again."

"And now?" Dr. Chen asked.

"Now I see that the person who 'left' me was fighting to stay. The abandonment wasn't a choice; it was a tragedy. There's a difference." I looked up, and for the first time in months, the world didn't feel like it was tilting to the right. "I've spent my life looking for a man to tell me I'm whole because I thought my mother told me I was nothing. But she didn't. She told me I was her reason for everything."

"That is a significant breakthrough, Eve," Dr. Chen said, her voice softening. "Your Grandmother never told you that your mother was trying to get back to you?"

"She did, she always told me, but I thought that was something she was telling me to make me feel better about the loss of my mother."

How does that change your view of the present? Of Sebastian? Of

Cam?"

I thought about Cam — the way he looked at me like I was the only thing in a crowded room. I'd always been afraid of that look. Worried, it was just another cage. But Cam knew about the struggle. He knew about the work of becoming. "It means I don't have to be a victim of my history anymore," I said. "I can forgive her. And maybe I can start to forgive myself for all the ways I tried to disappear just to survive."

The session ended, but the lightness stayed. I walked out into Bed-Stuy, the street noise rising around me. I felt like a woman who had finally found the map to her own heart — only to discover the treasure had been there all along, under all that damn grief.

I reached into my pocket and felt my phone buzz. A message from Cam: Thinking of you. How's Grandma doing?

I smiled from deep; it wasn't a reflex. I didn't deflect or half-answer. I told him the truth. She's getting better, and I think, finally, so am I.

The brownstone glowed in the late afternoon light, red bricks warm. It wasn't a prison or a museum; it was a home. And as I climbed the steps, I understood something: the paper trails didn't lead to a dead end. They led to a beginning.

Chapter 16

CONFRONTATIONS AND CONFESSIONS

The brownstone looked the same as it always had — solid, enduring, a testament to my grandmother's stubbornness. I'd been sleeping in my old room for two weeks while redecorating the garden level apartment, and we'd been dancing around the real conversation. The one about my choices, about Cam, about the wreckage I'd made of my marriage.

I couldn't put it off anymore.

Grandma Locust was in the kitchen when I came downstairs, working dough for her biscuits. Morning light caught the silver in her hair. She looked up when I walked in, and whatever was on my face told her this wasn't going to be small talk.

"Sit down, baby," she said, wiping her hands on her apron. "I'll make us some tea."

I sat at the kitchen table — the same one where I'd done homework, eaten a thousand meals, where my mother and uncle had eaten at as children. This table held everything.

Grandma set two cups of bush tea in front of us and eased into her chair with a soft grunt. She was better after the stroke, it didn't leave her with any permanent disabilities, but her arthritis had been flaring, but she'd never say so.

"You've been carrying something heavy," she said. She wasn't asking. "I can see it in the way you move. You want to talk about it?"

I wrapped both hands around the mug. "Grams, I need to tell you something. About Sebastian, about everything. The whole truth."

She nodded, dark eyes steady. "I'm listening."

"I was having an affair," I said, and the words just tumbled out. "Before Sebastian tried to kill me, I was sleeping with Camden. It had been going on for months."

I watched her face for a sign of judgment, disappointment, anger.

Her expression stayed neutral. Patient.

"I know, baby," she said softly.

My head came up. "You know? How?"

"I'm old, not blind," she said, a small smile. "I saw the way you looked when you talked about him. The way you lit up. And I saw the way you dimmed when Sebastian was around. A grandmother knows these things."

My eyes burned. "Then why didn't you say anything?"

"Because you weren't ready to hear it. Sometimes people need to walk their own path, make their own mistakes, before they're ready to listen to wisdom." She reached across and took my hand. "But I'm here now, and you're ready. So, talk."

I took a shaky breath. "I don't know why I did it, Grams. Or maybe I do and I'm just ashamed to admit it. Sebastian was suffocating. He watched every move, questioned everything. And Cam — Cam made me feel free. Like I could breathe again."

"And you think that justifies the affair?" she asked. Not unkindly.

"No," I said quickly. "I know it doesn't. I should have left Sebastian first. Should have been honest. But I was scared. Scared of being alone, scared of failing again, scared of proving that I'm just as broken as I feel."

Grandma Locust squeezed my hand. "Baby, let me tell you something. We all make choices we're not proud of. Every single one of us. The question isn't whether you made a mistake — you did. The question is what you're going to do about it now."

"I don't know," I said. "I'm in therapy, trying to understand myself, why I do what I do. But Grams, I feel so guilty. Not just about the affair — about everything. About pushing you away when you tried to help. About being so desperate for love that I married a man who turned out to be a monster."

"Stop," Grandma Locust said firmly. "Stop right there. Your mama's death was not your fault. You were just a baby when she passed. You didn't have any control over that."

My throat tightened.

"But the rest of it..." I said softly.

"The affair was wrong," she said, flat. "I'm not going to sugarcoat that. You made a choice that hurt people, broke vows you made. But

Evie, that doesn't make you irredeemable. It makes you human."

I wiped my eyes. "How can you not be disappointed in me?"

"Oh, baby, I am disappointed," she said, and it stung even though I'd been waiting for it. "I'm disappointed that you didn't value yourself enough to leave a bad situation before seeking comfort somewhere else. I'm disappointed you didn't come to me when you were struggling. But disappointed doesn't mean I don't love you. It doesn't mean I've given up on you."

"I don't deserve your love," I whispered.

"Love isn't about deserving," Grandma Locust said, gentle and firm at once. "Love is about choosing. Every day, I choose to love you. Not because you're perfect — Lord knows none of us are — but because you're mine. You're my grandbaby, and nothing you do will ever change that."

The tears came then, the kind that shake your whole body. Grandma Locust came around the table and pulled me in the way she had when I was small — cinnamon, the smell of home.

"Let it out," she murmured, rubbing my back. "Let it all out."

When I finally got myself together enough to talk, I pulled back and looked at her. "Why was I so drawn to Cam, Grams? Dr. Chen says I was looking for something in him that I need to find in myself, but I don't understand what that means."

She returned to her seat, wrapping both hands around her cup before taking a slow sip of tea.

"Camden represents something simple," she said. "A feeling you've been chasing for a long time. Not him, exactly... but how he makes you feel."

I frowned. "Which is what?" "Safe," she said. "Seen. Chosen."

The word settled heavy between us.

"You didn't grow up with steady love, Evie. Not because you weren't loved — you were — but because so much of it was taken from you too early. Your father left before you were even born. Your mama..." She paused gently. "You lost her before you could even understand what that meant."

I swallowed hard.

"So, when someone makes you feel chosen," she continued softly,

"it feels like everything."

"That still doesn't make it right," I said.

"No," she said. "It doesn't. But it helps you understand it."

She went quiet for a moment, her gaze drifting somewhere far away.

"I know what it feels like to be left," she added.

I looked up. "Grams..."

"Your grandfather," she said, her voice steady but distant. "We built a life together. Or at least I thought we did. Then one day he came home and told me he'd met someone else. A woman from the factory where he worked. Said he hadn't planned it, like that was supposed to make it easier."

My chest tightened. I'd heard this before, but it felt different today for some reason.

"He left," she continued. "Just like that. Walked out of the house, walked out on our kids, out of the life we built. Left me standing there trying to understand how something that felt so real could disappear so fast."

"I'm sorry, Grams," I said softly.

"I was angry for a long time," she admitted. "Hurt. Confused. Thought maybe if I had been better, prettier, quieter... he would've stayed."

Her eyes finally met mine.

"But that kind of thinking will eat you alive if you let it."

A quiet settled between us.

"Years later, I met Mr. Lewis," she said, her voice softening. "And he loved me in a way that didn't make me question myself. Didn't make me feel like I had to compete or prove my worth."

She leaned forward slightly.

"That's what I want for you, Evie. Not something that fills a hole for a moment... but something that's whole on its own."

I let that sit with me.

"But I can't go back," I said.

"No, you can't. None of us can. But Evie, you don't need to go back. You need to go forward. Figure out who you are now, today, with all your scars and all your wisdom. And then decide what kind of life you want to build."

"What if I don't know who I am? What if I've been acting for so long that now I can't remember who I really am?

Grandma Locust smiled — a knowing smile with decades behind it. "Then you start small. You remember what you loved before the world told you who to be. You remember your dreams before they got buried under other people's expectations. And you give yourself permission to want things, to need things, to be imperfect."

"After your grandfather left me, I took the kids back home to Beaufort with me for a few weeks. I was a mess and couldn't tend to them by myself. I was just too heartbroken. My mama sat me down one day and said something I've never forgotten. She said, 'Baby girl, you can't start the next chapter of your life if you keep re-reading the last one.' And I realized she was right. I was so busy mourning what I'd lost I couldn't see what was right in front of me. My children, who needed me."

"So... how did you move on?" I asked.

"It took time," she said. "I had to find my way back to myself first. Learn how to stand on my own again before I could let anybody else in."

"And then you met Mr. Lewis?"

She smiled softly. "Years later. I did. And it wasn't fireworks and passion like it had been with James. It was something quieter, steadier. Lewis loved me with his whole heart, and he showed me every single day through his actions. He was patient with my healing, gentle with my broken pieces. And eventually, I fell in love with him too. A different kind of love, but no less real."

I took that in. Saw the parallels clearly. "Do you think that's what

Cam and I could have? That steady kind of love?"

"I think," Grandma Locust said carefully, "that you need to figure out who you are before you can figure out who you want to be with. Camden is a good man, and he clearly loves you. But Evie, you can't build a healthy relationship on a broken foundation. You need to heal first."

"That's what Dr. Chen says too."

"Then she's a smart woman. Listen to her. Do the work. It won't be easy, baby. Healing never is. But it's worth it. I promise you, it's worth it."

We sat in comfortable silence for a moment, sipping our tea. Outside, the neighborhood was coming to life — children, cars, someone's radio in the distance.

"Grams," I said finally. "Can I ask you something?"

"Anything."

"Do you think I'm capable of real love? The kind you had with Mr.

Lewis. Or am I too damaged?"

She set down her cup and looked at me with such intensity that I almost looked away. "Eve Marie, you listen to me. You are not damaged. You are wounded, and there's a difference. Damaged things are broken beyond repair. Wounded things can heal. And yes, you are absolutely capable of real love. But first, you need to learn to love yourself."

"I don't know how to do that."

"You start by forgiving yourself," she said. "For the affair, for the mistakes, for being human. You treat yourself with the same compassion you'd show a friend. You start by believing you're worthy of good things, even when you don't feel like you are."

"What if I can't?"

"Then you fake it until you make it," she said, with a small smile. "You act like you believe it, and eventually your heart catches up with your actions. That's what I did after James left. I didn't believe I could love again, but I acted like I could. I went on dates with Lewis, let him court me, opened my heart even though I was terrified. And one day I realized I wasn't pretending anymore."

I turned that over — the idea of acting my way into healing, choosing to believe in my own worth even when everything inside me said otherwise.

"I'm scared, Grams," I admitted. "I'm scared of doing the work and finding out there's nothing worth saving. I'm scared of being alone. I'm scared of making the same mistakes again."

"Fear is normal," she said. "But don't let it paralyze you. Feel the fear and do it anyway. That's courage, baby. Not the absence of fear, but the willingness to move forward despite it."

"Will you help me?" My voice went small. "Will you be there while

I figure this out?"

"Baby, I'm not going anywhere," she said, reaching for my hand. "I'll be right here, every step. When you stumble, I'll help you up. When you doubt yourself, I'll remind you of your strength. That's what family does."

I squeezed her hand, and something in my chest loosened. I'd been so afraid of her disappointment, I'd forgotten the most important thing: Grandma Locust loved me unconditionally. Not because I was perfect.

Because I was hers.

"Thank you," I whispered. "For not giving up on me."

"Never," she said. "Now, let's finish these biscuits. Cooking always helps me think clearly, and I suspect you could use some of that clarity too."

I stood and joined her at the counter, hands in the dough alongside hers. We'd done this together a hundred times. Today it felt different.

We worked in comfortable silence, and I thought about everything she'd said. About forgiveness. About the difference between damaged and wounded. About my Granddaddy James and Mr. Lewis, about finding love again after heartbreak.

Maybe I could too. Maybe, with time and patience, I could become someone new. Not who I was before the pain — someone stronger, wiser, more honest with herself.

It wouldn't be quick. Dr. Chen had told me that from the start — healing isn't linear, setbacks are part of it. But for the first time since Sebastian tried to kill me, I thought maybe I could find my way through.

"Grams?" I said as we slid the biscuits into the oven.

"Yes, baby?"

"I love you."

She smiled, eyes crinkling at the corners. "I love you too, Evie. More than you'll ever know."

Standing in her kitchen with flour on my hands and the smell of baking filling the room, I believed her. I believed I was loved. That I was worthy. That I could heal.

It was enough. For now, it was enough.

Chapter 17

A SOVEREIGN SOUL

The drive into Bedminster felt like descending into a vacuum where the air had been filtered through silk. The gates of the High Ridge Country Club didn't open — they retreated, yielding to my modest sedan with mechanical resentment. Everything here was curated to a degree that made nature look like an intruder. The lawns were a chemical green, mowed into geometric precision — I half-expected them to bleed neon if one blade went astray. The kind of place where silence had a price tag, and the only sound was the distant thwack of a tennis ball being punished by someone with a legacy and a trust fund.

I parked among the German-engineered steel and sat there a moment, hands on the wheel until my knuckles went pale. I caught myself in the rearview mirror. Wild curls traded for a sleek low bun, face a mask of neutral, expensive-looking makeup. I looked like the woman Sebastian had always wanted me to be — a ghost of the wife who'd nearly drowned in a tub of gardenias and poisoned wine. But underneath the silk blouse and tailored slacks, my heart was beating steadily and heavy. I wasn't here as a supplicant. I was here as a witness to my own survival.

Inside, the clubhouse smelled of floor wax, gin, and the quiet desperation of people who'd never heard the word "no." A porter walked me to the terrace, footsteps echoing on polished flagstone. Arthur and Beatrice Whitmore were already seated at a corner table with a view of the eighteenth green. They looked like the blueprints Sebastian had been built from. Arthur: deep brown skin, charcoal wool and silver hair, a face of calculated stoicism. Beatrice: pearls and Botox, two chips of frozen Atlantic blue for eyes, already sorting my value before I cleared the last step.

"Eve," Arthur said, rising just an inch, it was just from protocol, not warmth.

"Thank you for coming. We know the city can be... taxing."

"It's good to see you, Arthur. Beatrice," I said. I planned to be level and cool-headed, we'd never had much to say to each other. I'd practiced that voice in the mirror for three days. I sat down, the wrought-iron chair scraping stone. A waiter materialized instantly with Earl Grey, as though he'd anticipated my exact thirst. The steam curled up like cold mist.

Beatrice cut straight through any choreography of small talk. She leaned forward, her annoyingly gawdy diamonds sparkling.

"We've followed the news, of course. The allegations. The spectacle. It's been a very difficult time for our family name, Eve. And for you, I imagine, given your... history."

That word dropped into the center of the table like a stone. She meant the pills. The "restlessness" Sebastian had documented so carefully. The "instability" they planned to use as a shield. I felt the phantom weight of a bottle in my palm; it was muscle memory. I reached for the tea instead. She wants you to feel small. She wants you to feel like a broken thing that needs managing.

"It has been a difficult time," I agreed, watching a hawk circle high above the fairway. "Surviving a murder attempt generally is." I looked them each in the eyes deliberately.

Arthur cleared his throat; it sounded dry and scratchy.

"We prefer to think of it as a profound misunderstanding, Eve. Sebastian has always been... intense. High-functioning men often suffer under the weight of their own expectations. And you were struggling. The toxicology report showed quite a cocktail in your system. Any jury would see a woman who was reaching for an exit, and a husband who perhaps moved too slowly to stop her."

Seamless. A family tradition of gaslighting, these fuckers passed down like a signet ring. They weren't just defending their son — they were rewriting physics to fit the narrative. To them, the poison wasn't a crime. It was a line item in a marriage that had gone over budget.

"He forged my signature on a five-million-dollar life insurance policy, Arthur," I said, dropping my voice an octave. "He watched me drown. There is no misunderstanding that bridges the gap between a glass of wine and a body in a tub."

Beatrice reached into her handbag and produced a heavy cream envelope. She slid it across the table the same way Sebastian used to slide me my "medicine."

"We aren't here to litigate the past, Eve. We are here to secure the future," she said.

"Sebastian is our only son. We will not see him languish in a cell because of a domestic tragedy fueled by your own dependencies. Inside that envelope is a settlement. Seven figures. Enough to ensure you never have to work a day in your life. Enough to move back to Brooklyn, or anywhere else your little heart desires."

She paused. Her gaze dropped to my midsection and stayed there; I guess she was deep in thought about her future grandchild.

"With Jada, in her condition...for the child. A Whitmore heir deserves a certain standard of living, wouldn't you agree? Private schools. Travel. A life far away from the grit of Bed-Stuy." She smirked. "Why don't you let our son come home and be a father to his child with Jada."

"He knew she was pregnant before he tried it, he should've thought about their kid. That's not my fucking problem!"

I opened the envelope. The numbers on the check were dizzying — a long string of zeros promising effortless safety. For a split second, the old Eve wavered. I thought of the dated walls of Grandma Locust's brownstone, the work of opening the dance center, the exhaustion that lived in my bones every night. I could take the money. Buy a house on the water and fade into the background of someone else's story. Tell the court it was an accident. Say I was confused, that the pills had clouded things, that Sebastian was just a man trying to help a broken woman.

Arthur was smiling. Thin and satisfied, certain he'd already won.

He saw me as a transaction to be settled and archived.

You're everything to me, Sebastian's voice said in my head, breath smelling of peppermint and control. The money was just another little blue pill. A way to make the bars look like ribbons again. If I signed that check, I'd be sliding back under the water — not of the body this time, but of spirit. Back in the tub. Letting the Whitmore legacy wash over me until I disappeared.

They would have to banter with Jada when it came to Sebastian. I was done. I could use the money, but I learned the hard way, that peace and truth was something you traded for a view of a golf course.

I slid the check back into the envelope. Tucked the flap in slowly, deliberately. Pushed it back across the table. The motion felt like moving a mountain.

"No," I said.

Beatrice blinked. First crack in the composure. "I don't think you understand, Eve. This is a very generous offer. More than you could ever earn in your life."

"I understand perfectly," I said, leaning in until I was just inches from her face. "You want to buy my silence because you're afraid of what my voice will do to your name. You want to paint me as an addict and Sebastian as the savior because the truth is too ugly for your country club. But my silence isn't for sale. Not for seven figures. Not for seventy."

Arthur's mask fell. The statesman gone, the predator underneath. "Be careful, Eve. We have resources. We have lawyers who can make your life a living hell. We can bring up every pill you ever took, every night you spent in Brooklyn with that... convict. We can make sure you lose everything."

The threat was supposed to break me. Instead, it felt almost clarifying — the final, desperate move of people who'd realized they'd lost their grip. I thought of Cam, cinnamon-brown skin and the way he looked at me like I was the only light in the room. I thought of Grandma Locust in her kitchen, telling me to find my own path. I thought of the dance studio, the sweat, the feeling of my body moving for me alone.

"You can try," I said, standing. "Drag my name through the mud, tell the world I'm a mess. I'll still be standing in that courtroom. I'll look at the judge, and I'll look at your son, and I'll tell them exactly what happened in that bathroom. I'll tell them how he watched me die, and I'll tell them how I chose to live."

I looked at the envelope one last time. It looked small now.

Insignificant. Trash on a perfect lawn.

"Keep your money, Arthur. Use it to pay for Sebastian's defense. He's going to need every penny," I said. I didn't wait for a response. I turned and walked, my heels striking the flagstone — a rhythm that felt like a heartbeat. A real, sovereign one.

The porter reached for the door. I beat him to it, pulled the heavy wood open myself.

Out into the bright, blinding Jersey sun. The air was still thin, still filtering but as I got in the car and turned the key, I rolled all the windows down. I wanted the wind, the noise, the grit. I wanted everything that didn't belong to the Whitmore's.

Driving past the manicured lawns and the silent geometric grass, the world didn't tilt. It stayed perfectly, beautifully level. I was Eve Whitmore, and for the first time in my life, I was the only person who owned me.

Chapter 18

THE TRIAL AND ITS AFTERMATH

The courthouse was everything I'd imagined and worse—cold, imposing, fluorescent lights that made everyone look slightly ill. I sat in the gallery between Grandma Locust and Cam. Cam's phone buzzed in his pocket—his shop foreman, again—and he left it there, though I could see his jaw working. My hands were clasped so tight my knuckles were pale.

Sebastian was led in wearing a dark, well-tailored suit, his hands cuffed in front of him. He was thinner than I remembered, gaunt, dark circles eating up most of his face. For a moment—just a moment—I felt something that might have been pity. Then I remembered the drugs burning through my system, the moment I understood I was dying, and it was gone.

"All rise," the bailiff announced, and we stood as Judge Morrison entered. Black woman, who looked to be in her sixties, with an air of absolute no-nonsense authority that made the whole room pull itself together.

The proceedings began. I tried to track the legal language, the formal procedures, but my mind kept sliding off them. I watched Sebastian's lawyer—slick, expensive suit—argue that his client had acted under extreme emotional duress, that he'd made a terrible mistake but didn't deserve the maximum sentence.

Then the prosecutor, a sharp woman named Angela Rodriguez, laid out the evidence. Life insurance policy, text messages, the toxicology report. But the room shifted when she produced the silver drive, I'd found—the Aegis files. Ms. Rodriguez called the federal agents forward to authenticate the encrypted data, and it came out: Sebastian hadn't been looking for an insurance payout. He'd been brokering a five-million-dollar deal with a foreign interest. I wasn't just a wife he'd grown tired of. I was the only witness who could place the stolen drive in his hands, which made my murder a line item in a federal espionage deal. He wasn't a husband looking for a way out. He was a corporate spy removing liability. The premeditation was clear. Undeniable.

Then Jada was called to the stand. She wasn't the defiant mistress I'd imagined, and she wasn't the cold-eyed co-conspirator the early police reports had painted. She was the prosecution's star witness now, here under a fragile plea agreement that had traded her testimony for a suspended sentence. She was starting to show—the rounding of her fourth month visible beneath her conservative dress. The baby that should have been a blessing.

As she testified about Sebastian's plans, about how he'd promised her a future together once I was out of the picture, I watched her carefully. Red-rimmed swollen eyes, a trembling voice, she looked genuinely broken. Part of me wanted to hate her, to blame her for everything. But another part—the part that'd been learning about manipulation in therapy—

recognized she'd been hollowed out by the same man. An accessory by law, a casualty by design.

Sebastian had manipulated her the same way he'd manipulated me. He'd promised love and security while planning to use insurance money from my death to fund their new life. She'd been complicit, yes, but she'd also been deceived.

When the prosecutor asked if she'd known about Sebastian's plan to kill me, Jada broke down completely.

"I didn't know," she sobbed. "I swear I didn't know. He told me he was going to divorce her, that we'd be together. I never thought... I never imagined he would try to kill her."

The prosecutor pressed harder. "But you knew about the life insurance policy?"

"Yes," Jada admitted, her voice barely audible. "But he spoke about the Aegis drive—a five-million-dollar deal he was brokering with a foreign interest—and said the insurance was just to ensure our liquid security while we moved abroad. He told me the drive was the real prize, but that he needed to resolve his 'domestic liabilities' before we could leave. I didn't realize he meant Eve."

"And the text messages where you discussed what you'd do with the money after Ms. Whitmore's death?"

"I thought it was hypothetical," Jada insisted. "Like a fantasy. I didn't think he was actually planning it."

I didn't know if I believed her. Maybe she really had been that naive. Maybe she'd chosen not to look because the fantasy was too good. Either way, she was paying for it now. Her marriage was wreckage, her reputation a smear of tabloid ink, and her freedom was tethered to the truth she told today. The prosecutor had made it clear: full cooperation or a cell of her own.

Ms. Rodriguez wasn't done. She approached the witness stand with a manila folder, heels clicking against the marble floor, the sound echoing through the silent courtroom.

"Ms. Jennings, let's talk about the timeline of your affair with Mr. Whitmore." Ms. Rodriguez's voice was calm but firm. "When exactly did it begin?"

Jada dabbed at her eyes, smudging her mascara further. "About eighteen months ago. Maybe longer. It's hard to remember exactly."

"Eighteen months," Ms. Rodriguez repeated, letting the words hang. "That's a year and a half. During that time, how often did you and Mr. Whitmore see each other?"

"Two, sometimes three times a week." Jada's voice was barely above a whisper.

"And where did these meetings take place?"

"Hotels, mostly. Sometimes his office after hours. Once or twice at my house when Derek was traveling."

My stomach turned. My house. The apartment Sebastian and I shared. Had he brought her there too? I gripped the edge of the bench, knuckles white, if she would've said my apartment, it would take the entire row of my support system to hold me back from running up there and slapping her, pregnant and all.

Ms. Rodriguez consulted her notes. "Ms. Jennings, I'm going to read you a text message from your phone, dated March 15th of this year.

You wrote to Mr. Whitmore: 'Once she's gone, we can finally be together. No more hiding. No more lies. Just us and the life we deserve.' Do you remember sending that message?"

Jada's face crumpled. "Yes."

"What did you mean by 'once she's gone'?"

"I thought... I thought he meant divorce. That once the divorce was final, we could be together openly."

"But Mr. Whitmore never filed for divorce, did he?"

"No."

"In fact, according to his attorney's records, he never even consulted with a divorce lawyer. Isn't that correct?"

"I... I don't know. He told me he was handling it."

Ms. Rodgriguez pulled out another document. "Let's talk about the life insurance policy. When did Mr. Whitmore first mention it to you?"

Jada shifted in her seat, twisting the tissue into shreds. "Maybe six months ago? He said he'd increased Eve's policy to two million dollars, he didn't tell me it was five. He said it was smart financial planning, that all successful couples did it."

"And what was your reaction?"

"I didn't think much of it at the time. Derek and I have life insurance policies too. It seemed normal."

"But then Mr. Whitmore started talking about what you'd do with the money, didn't he?"

Jada nodded, tears streaming down her face. "Yes."

"Can you tell the court what he said?"

"He said..." Jada's voice broke. "He said we could travel. Buy a house in the Hamptons. Start fresh somewhere new. He made it sound like a dream."

"Did he ever explicitly say he was going to kill his wife?"

"No. Never. He just kept saying 'when Eve's gone' or 'after Eve.' I thought he meant after the divorce."

Ms. Rodriguez's expression hardened. "Ms. Jennings, you're an intelligent woman. You have a master's degree in business administration. You work in strategic finance. Are you really asking this court to believe that you didn't understand what 'when Eve's gone' meant in the context of a two-million-dollar life insurance policy?"

"Objection!" Sebastian's defense attorney, Mr. Caldwell, shot to his feet. "Argumentative."

"Sustained," the judge said. "Rephrase, Ms. Rodriguez."

Ms. Rodriguez nodded. "Ms. Jennings, looking back now, do you believe Mr. Whitmore was planning to kill his wife?"

"Yes," Jada whispered. "Yes, I do."

"And when did you first suspect this?"

"When I heard about the poisoning. When the police came to question me. That's when everything clicked into place—all the conversations, the texts, the way he talked about the future. I realized I'd been so blinded by what I wanted that I didn't see what was right in front of me."

I watched Jada as she spoke. For the first time, I saw past my anger. Sebastian had a gift for making you believe what he wanted you to believe, for bending reality until you couldn't tell truth from lies. She hadn't escaped that any more than I had.

Ms. Rodriguez returned to her table and picked up another document. "Ms. Jennings, I'm going to show you a series of text messages between you and Mr. Whitmore from April 20th, just three days before the poisoning. In these messages, you discuss meeting at a hotel. You write: 'I can't wait to start our real life together.' And he responds: 'Soon, baby. Very soon. Everything's falling into place.' What did you understand 'everything's falling into place' to mean?" Jada's hands trembled. "I thought he meant the divorce was progressing. That he was getting his affairs in order."

"But there was no divorce proceeding, was there?"

"No."

"So, what was 'falling into place,' Ms. Jennings?"

Jada looked directly at me for the first time since taking the stand. Eyes red, face blotchy with tears. "His plan to kill her," she said, her voice breaking. "His plan to kill Eve."

The courtroom erupted. The judge banged on her gavel, calling for order.

Ms. Rodriguez let the moment settle, let what she just say marinade a bit. "Ms. Jennings, how did you feel when you learned that Eve

Whitmore had been poisoned?"

"Horrified. Sick. I couldn't believe it. I kept thinking it had to be a mistake, that Sebastian couldn't have actually done it."

"But the evidence suggests otherwise, doesn't it?"

"Yes."

"And when the police questioned you, you initially lied about the affair, didn't you?"

Jada nodded miserably. "Yes. I was scared. Derek knew we were having an affair, and about the baby, but I didn’t want him to hear about this, not something so extreme like this. I didn't want to lose everything."

"But you eventually told the truth?"

"Yes. My attorney advised me to cooperate fully. And I wanted to. I wanted to make things right, even though I knew it was too late."

Ms. Rodriguez paused. "Ms. Jennings, do you believe you bear any responsibility for what happened to Eve Whitmore?"

"Objection!" Mr. Caldwell was on his feet again. "Calls for speculation."

"Your Honor, the witness' state of mind is relevant to establishing Mr. Whitmore's manipulation tactics," Ms. Rodriguez argued.

"I'll allow it," the judge said. "But keep it brief."

Jada looked down at her hands. "Yes. I do. If I hadn't been involved with Sebastian, if I hadn't encouraged his fantasies about our future together, maybe he wouldn't have... maybe Eve would be okay."

"But you didn't poison her, did you?"

"No."

"You didn't plan to poison her?"

"No."

"Sebastian Whitmore acted alone in his attempt to murder his wife, correct?"

"Yes."

"Thank you, Ms. Jennings. No further questions."

I felt Cam's hand find mine as Ms. Rodriguez returned to her seat. I squeezed it. Across the aisle, Sebastian sat perfectly still, his face looked like a closed door. How had I ever thought I knew this man?

Mr. Caldwell rose slowly, buttoning his suit jacket. You could tell the Whitmore's paid top dollar for his expertise. Older than Ms. Rodriguez, silver hair, a grandfatherly demeanor he wore like a costume. He approached Jada with a slight smile.

"Ms. Jennings, that was quite a performance," he began.

"Objection!" Ms. Rodriguez called out.

"Withdrawn." Mr. Caldwell's smile didn't waver. "Ms. Jennings, you testified that you and my client were having an affair for approximately eighteen months, correct?"

"Yes."

"And during that time, you were also married to Derek Jennings, a business partner of my client?"

"Yes."

"So, you're comfortable with deception, aren't you? With lying to people who trust you?"

Jada flinched. "I'm not proud of what I did."

"But you did it, nonetheless. You lied to your husband for eighteen months. You snuck around behind his back. You betrayed his trust.

Isn't that correct?"

"Yes."

"And you lied to the police initially when they questioned

you about the affair, didn't you?"

"Yes, but"

"A simple yes or no will suffice, Ms. Jennings." Mr. Caldwell's voice went sharp, the grandfatherly act slipping. "You lied to the police. You lied to your husband. You've admitted to being a liar. So why should this jury believe anything you say now?"

"Because I'm telling the truth now," Jada said, voice stronger. "I know I made mistakes. Terrible mistakes. But I'm not lying about

Sebastian."

"Aren't you?" Mr. Caldwell pulled out his own set of documents.

"Ms. Jennings, isn't it true that you initiated the affair with my client?" "I... we were in love with each other forever, since we were young.

It wasn't one-sided."

"But you made the first move to re-engage in your relationship, didn't you? You sent him suggestive text messages. You invited him to meet you for drinks. You pursued him."

"It wasn't like that."

"Then how was it, Ms. Jennings? Because the text messages I have here paint a very different picture. Let me read one from you, dated November 3rd, two years ago: 'I can't stop thinking about you. Meet me tonight. I need to see you.' Does that sound like someone who was being pursued, or someone doing the pursuing?"

Jada's face flushed. "I always loved Sebastian and he loved me too. If it weren't for his parents, we would've been married and we wouldn't be here today! He wanted the affair as much as I did."

"Did he? Or did you seduce a married man, manipulate him with promises and fantasies, and then when things went wrong, decide to save yourself by blaming him for everything?"

"No! That's not what happened!"

"Isn't it?" Mr. Caldwell leaned against the witness stand, voice dropping. "Ms. Jennings, I think you've been manipulative since you were both teens, you testified that you discussed the life insurance policy with my client. You discussed what you'd do with the money. You sent text messages about starting a new life together. Doesn't that make you complicit in any plan to harm Mrs. Whitmore?"

"I didn't know he was going to hurt her!"

"But you benefited from the idea of her being 'gone,' didn't you? You wanted her out of the picture so you could have Sebastian to yourself."

"I wanted him to divorce her, not kill her!"

"But you never discouraged him when he talked about the insurance money, did you? You never said, 'Sebastian, this is wrong. You need to get a divorce like a normal person.' You went along with it because you wanted the money too."

"That's not true!"

"Isn't it?" Mr. Caldwell pulled out another document. "Ms. Jennings, I have here a credit card statement from your account showing purchases at a real estate office in the Hamptons. You were looking at houses, weren't you? Houses you planned to buy with the insurance money?"

Jada's face went pale. "I... I was just looking. It was a fantasy.

I never thought—"

"You never thought you'd get caught," Mr. Caldwell finished. "You never thought the police would trace the poisoning back to my client, and by extension, back to you. So now you're here, trying to save yourself by painting my client as a monster and yourself as an innocent victim."

"I am a victim!" Jada's voice rose. "Sebastian manipulated me. He made me believe we had a future together, that we would be a family!

He used me!"

"Or did you use him, Ms. Jennings? Did you see a wealthy, successful man and decide you wanted him for yourself? Did you seduce him, manipulate him, and then when his wife nearly died, decide to throw him under the bus to save your own skin?"

"No!" Jada was crying openly now. "I loved him. I thought he loved me. I didn't know he was capable of murder."

"But you were capable of adultery. Of lying. Of betrayal. So, forgive me if I find your sudden moral clarity a bit convenient." "Objection!" Ms. Rodriguez was on her feet. "Counsel is badgering the witness."

"Sustained," the judge said. "Mr. Caldwell, move on."

Mr. Caldwell nodded, satisfaction flickering behind his eyes. He'd done what he came to do, make Jada look like a liar and a schemer, planted doubt about her testimony.

"Ms. Jennings, one final question," Mr. Caldwell said. "You testified that my client never explicitly told you he was going to kill his wife. Is that correct?"

"Yes."

"So, everything you've said today about his 'plan' is based on your interpretation of his words and actions, correct? Your assumptions about what he meant?"

"I... yes, but..."

I felt the surge of anger as Mr. Caldwell returned to his seat. He'd twisted everything, made Jada look like the villain when Sebastian was the one who'd tried to kill me. But I understood his strategy—create reasonable doubt. Make the jury question whether Sebastian had really planned to murder me or if it was all just talk, just fantasy.

Ms. Rodriguez stood for redirect. "Ms. Jennings, Mr. Caldwell suggested that you manipulated his client. But isn't it true that Sebastian Whitmore is a successful businessman who's been negotiating deals and managing people for over a decade?"

"Yes."

"So, he's not exactly naive or easily manipulated, is he?"

"No. Sebastian is very intelligent. Very calculating."

"And when he talked about the insurance money, about your future together, did he seem confused or uncertain?"

"No. He seemed confident. Like he had everything planned out."

"Did he ever express guilt or remorse about his wife?"

Jada hesitated. "No. He talked about her like she was an obstacle.

Something in his way."

"And when you suggested he get a divorce, what did he say?"

"He said divorce was too expensive. Too complicated. That there was an easier way."

"Did you understand what he meant by 'an easier way'?"

"At the time, I didn't let myself think about it. But looking back... yes. I think I knew what he meant. I just didn't want to believe it."

Ms. Rodriguez nodded. "Ms. Jennings, you've admitted to making mistakes. To lying. To having an affair. But are you lying now about Sebastian Whitmore's intentions?"

"No." Jada looked directly at the jury. "I'm telling the truth. Sebastian planned to kill his wife. And I was too blinded by what I wanted to see until it was too late."

"Thank you, Ms. Jennings. No further questions."

When Jada stepped down from the witness stand, she had to walk past our side of the courtroom. Our eyes met. I saw it all—guilt, shame, regret, and something else. Recognition. She saw herself in me, and I saw myself in her. Two women who'd loved the same man and paid the price.

I didn't smile. I didn't nod. But I didn't look away either. I held her gaze until she passed, because Jada wasn't my enemy. She was another casualty of Sebastian's design. He was the monster, the one who'd pulled us both into his orbit and let us burn. When they called for victim impact statements, I stood on shaking legs and walked to the front. I'd rewritten my statement a dozen times, but standing at that podium with Sebastian's eyes on me, every word I'd prepared disappeared.

"I trusted you," I said, voice barely above a whisper. The judge leaned forward. I cleared my throat. "I trusted you with my life, with my future, with my heart. And you tried to take all of that away from me."

Sebastian looked down.

"I keep asking myself why," I continued, voice steadying. "Why wasn't I enough? Why did you marry me if you were planning to kill me? Was any of it real, or was I just a means to an end from the beginning?"

"Ms. Whitmore," the judge said gently, "please continue."

"I've spent the last few months in therapy, trying to understand how I ended up here. Trying to figure out what I missed, what signs I ignored. And I've realized that this isn't about me. This is about you, Sebastian. About your choices, your greed, your complete disregard for human life."

I took a breath. "You didn't just try to kill me. You killed the woman I was. The woman who believed in love, who trusted easily, who saw the best in people. That woman is gone, and I'm still figuring out who I am without her."

Tears ran down my face and I left them there. Let him see it. Let everyone see.

"But here's what I want you to know," I said, looking directly at Sebastian for the first time. "You didn't win. I'm still here. I'm still standing. And I'm going to build a life that's so full of love and joy and purpose that you'll become nothing more than a footnote in my story. A cautionary tale about what happens when you mistake material things and control for love."

I walked back to my seat, legs still trembling. Cam squeezed my hand—there was copper dust on his thumb and a tiredness behind his eyes that had nothing to do with the trial. Grandma Locust whispered,

"Well done, baby."

Later, in the corridor outside the courtroom, while lawyers

shuffled papers and Grandma Locust accepted a glass of water from the bailiff, I caught Cam leaning against the wall alone. He was staring at his hands, those same hands that could thread copper pipe in the dark, that had held me together on the nights I couldn't hold myself. His jaw was tight. I'd seen that look before, on the nights he came home from a call-back job in a neighborhood he used to run, when the distance between who he was and who he'd been felt impossibly small. "You don't have to keep showing up for this," I said. He looked up. "Yes, I do," he said, and there was nothing romantic in his voice—just the plain, exhausted weight of a man who had decided. "Because if I don't, I spend the rest of my life being the guy who walked away from the only thing he ever got right." He pushed off the wall, straightened his jacket, and walked back through the courtroom doors before I could answer. I stood there for a moment, watching the space where he'd been, understanding for the first time that Cam's love wasn't easy or uncomplicated. It was chosen. Every single day. And so was mine.

He was waiting by my car when it was over. Cam was leaning against the door with his hands in his jacket pockets, watching the street. He looked tired in the way that has nothing to do with sleep — the tiredness that comes from carrying something heavy for a long time and refusing to put it down.

“You ate today?” he asked when I got close.

“No.”

He nodded like that was what he expected. “There’s a place two blocks from here. Come on.”

We didn’t talk about the trial. We sat in a corner booth in a Jamaican spot not too far from the courthouse with plates of oxtail and rice between us, and for a while neither of us said anything real. Then I put my fork down and looked at him.

"I need to ask you something and I need you to be honest with me."

He looked up. "Always."

"Why are you still here? And I don't mean today. I mean... all of it. The whole mess of me. The marriage, the pills, the trial. All the ways I wasn't who I should have been when I was with you the first time." I kept my eyes on him. "What is it you actually want from me,

Camden?"

He was quiet for a moment — not the silence of a man stalling, but the silence of a man who had already thought this through a thousand times and was choosing how much truth to hand over at once.

"I don't want anything from you, Eve." His voice was steady, unhurried. "I want something with you. There's a difference. I'm not here because I need you to complete something for me. I'm here because I know who you are when you're not performing. I've seen that version of you since we were fifteen, and I've never stopped wanting to be in a room with her."

I stared at the tablecloth. "I cheated on my husband with you."

"I know that."

"I lied to you too. About the timeline. About when things started."

"I know that too." He picked up his fork again, calm, unbothered. "You think I don't know you were a mess when you came back to me? Eve. I'm a grown man. I wasn't some accident that happened to you. I made my own choices. And I'd make them again."

Something in my chest cracked open, not in pieces but more like a window that had been painted shut for years, finally giving way. “I don’t want to be someone you rescue.”

“Good.” He met my eyes. “Because I don’t want to rescue you. I want to have dinner with you. I want to argue about what to watch on a Friday night and lose, which I will, because you always win. I want the regular, boring, beautiful stuff. That’s what I’m here for.”

I laughed, a real knee slapping hearty laugh, not just with my mouth in the shape of a laugh, but for the first time in longer than I could remember tears came to my eyes and it wasn’t from sadness.

We finished the food. He paid, and I let him, and we walked back out into the Jersey afternoon busyness with our shoulders close but not touching, the way you walk when you’re not sure yet but you’re not, not sure either. It was enough for now. It was more than enough.

The trial lasted three days. Three days of testimony, evidence, legal arguments. Three days of reliving the worst moment of my life, over and over. By the time closing arguments came, I was running on coffee and anger.

The jury deliberated for six hours. Finally, the bailiff announced they'd reached a verdict.

"On the counts of attempted murder in the first degree and federal corporate espionage, how do you find?" "Guilty on all counts."

Guilty. Guilty. Guilty.

I felt Cam's arm around me, felt Grandma Locust's hand in mine, but it all seemed far away, muffled. Sebastian showed nothing as the verdict was read, nothing as the judge scheduled sentencing for two weeks later, noting that the combination of attempted murder and the Economic Espionage Act violations would trigger mandatory minimums—he'd never see the sun as a free man again at least not as a young man.

As they led him away, he looked at me one last time. I'd expected anger, resentment. What I saw instead looked almost like regret.

Too little. Too late.

Outside, reporters swarmed with cameras and questions. Cam and Grandma Locust formed a wall around me as we pushed through to the car. I kept my head down. They didn't get to see my tears.

Once we were in Cam's car, the adrenaline that'd been holding me upright finally crashed. I slumped against the seat, my whole body shaking.

"It's over," Cam said softly, pulling out of the parking lot. He looked hollowed out—the strain of his struggling business and his mother's warnings about the baggage I'd brought into his life showing in the set of his shoulders. "It's finally over."

I leaned my head against the cold window, watching the courthouse shrink in the side mirror. The legal battle was won, the verdict locked in the record. But as we crossed the bridge back toward Brooklyn, I knew the quiet that followed would be its own kind of hard. The courtroom was behind me. The woman I still had to become was somewhere up ahead.

Chapter 19

FINDING MYSELF

Three months after the trial, I ended up in front of a dance studio in Greenpoint on a Thursday evening without entirely meaning to. I'd been walking — just walking, the way I'd started doing some evenings when the brownstone got too quiet and my thoughts got too loud. The studio was on the second floor of a converted townhouse, and I'd heard the music before I saw the sign: a deep, rolling bass line that moved through the floor of the building and up through the soles of my shoes, all the way into my chest.

I stood on the sidewalk and looked up at the lit windows. Bodies moving behind the glass. I could see the instructor's hands cutting through the air, counting, directing.

My mother was a dancer.

That thought hit me differently standing there than it had anywhere else. In therapy, on paper, in the trunk letters — I'd been piecing Dominique together intellectually, turning her into someone I could understand. But standing there with that bass in my sternum, I didn't understand her. I felt her. The girl from a nearby neighborhood had all that rhythm in her body and nowhere to put it, who had dreamed of the stage the way I'd dreamed of the trading floor. We'd both wanted something that required us to be fully alive. We'd both let someone convince us to shrink.

I hadn't danced since my junior year of college, before I met Bash, before I let what he thought I should do take priority over what I wanted to do. I had told myself I'd just stopped. But standing there, I understood that wasn't the truth. Sebastian had told me, early on, that he found dance performances "a little theatrical" — and I had laughed and agreed and somewhere in that agreement, filed my own joy away like an embarrassment. The way I'd filed away my natural hair. The way I'd filed away my appetite, my opinions, my volume. All of it folded up and put somewhere tidy so he could feel comfortable in the same room as me.

"You going in?"

A woman was standing beside me — I hadn't heard her come up. Mid-thirties, box braids high on her head, the kind of lean muscle you get from actually dancing and not from a gym. She was reading my face with the directness of someone who had stood on that same sidewalk herself once.

"I'm thinking about it," I said.

"First time?"

"First time in a long time. I used to dance. Before life got in the way."

She nodded like that was an answer she'd heard before and respected. "I'm Simone. I teach the class that's about to start. You should come up."

"I don't know if I'm—"

"Ready?" She smiled. "Nobody is. That's never actually the question. First class is free. Come on."

I followed her inside before the logical part of my brain could organize a reason not to.

The studio smelled like sweat and resin and effort — the smell of a space where people came to do the real thing. I pulled my sweatshirt over my head in the back and found a spot near the mirror. The other women in the class had the easy comfort of regulars: stretching and laughing and catching up across the room. I stood in my corner and stretched and tried not to feel like an imposter.

When the music started, my body became awkward immediately. Counted wrong. Stepped left when I should have stepped right. The woman next to me quietly mirrored the correct move without drawing attention to it, the kind of silent grace you only find in rooms full of Black women who have all been beginners at something, at some point and remember what that felt like.

And then, about twenty minutes in, something in me was released.

It wasn't that I suddenly knew the steps. I didn't. But I stopped fighting the music and started listening to it, and my body found the underneath of it the pulse, the pull — and something I hadn't felt in years moved through me like a key turning in a lock. Not talent, or grace, just freedom. The specific freedom of a body that is moving for itself and no one else.

I thought about Dominique, my sweet mama. I thought about her at seventeen, at twenty, on whatever stage she'd found before Marty found her. I thought about what it must have felt like to have this and then have it taken and replaced by a habit you have no control over. And I thought about how the studio I was going to build in her name was going to be a place where nobody had to lose this feeling. Where little girls from this neighborhood could come and move and be loud and be physical and be full and not one person would tell them it was too much or they were too much.

By the end of the class I was drenched, and my legs were gone and I was grinning in a way that felt almost embarrassing.

"You have it," Simone said when I was gathering my things. "Whatever it was before life got in the way, you still have it. Bodies hold onto the things that are really theirs."

I thought about that my entire walk home. Bodies hold onto the things that are really theirs.

Dominique's daughter, dancing in Greenpoint on a Thursday night.

Mama, I'm coming back for both of us.

That night I opened my journal. Dr. Chen had asked me to write about moments when I felt most like myself.

Today I danced, I wrote. I did it for me. For the first time in years, I moved my body because it asked me to and I said yes. I thought about my mother the whole time — not the mother who left, but the mother who was trying to come back. The dancer. The dreamer. I'm not broken. I'm just getting back what was always mine.

- ✧ -

The prison smelled of industrial cleaner and desperation. My hands trembled slightly as I walked through the metal detectors and handed over my ID. Dr. Chen had asked me if I needed closure with Sebastian, and I'd spent three sessions wrestling with the answer. Finally, I'd decided: yes. Not for him but for me.

The visitation room was stark—white walls, fluorescent lights, metal tables bolted to the floor. When Sebastian walked in wearing his orange jumpsuit, I barely recognized him. He'd lost weight, his face was gaunt and shadowed. I felt a flicker of something—not pity exactly, but acknowledgment of how far we'd both fallen.

"Eve." His voice cracked. "I didn't think you'd come."

"I almost didn't." I sat down, keeping my hands in my lap. "But I needed to hear it from you. Why, Sebastian? Why marry me if you were planning to kill me?"

He looked away, jaw working. "My parents threatened to cut me off if I didn't end things with Jada. Her father and mine had a falling out when we were young and in love, their business went south, and the trust between them evaporated. They said if I stayed with her, I'd lose everything." He finally met my eyes. "The life insurance was supposed to be my way out. Start over with Jada, away from their control."

I stared at him, waiting for the rage. All I felt was hollow. "So, you married me as a financial plan. And when that wasn't enough, you decided murder was easier than divorce."

"I was desperate..."

"You were selfish." My voice was steady now, clear. "You could have walked away. Filed for divorce. Dealt with your parents like an adult. Instead, you tried to kill someone who at some point loved you." I stood. "I came here hoping to understand. But there's nothing to understand, Sebastian. You made a choice. And now you're living with it."

"Eve, please."

"I forgive you," I said quietly. "Not because you deserve it, but because I deserve to be free of you. Completely."

I walked out without looking back.

The drive home felt surreal. I kept replaying Sebastian's words, his hollow justifications, the emptiness in his eyes. Dr. Chen was right; closure wasn't about getting answers. It was about accepting that some questions don't have satisfying ones.

When I climbed the steps to Grandma Locust's brownstone, Cam was sitting on the stoop, with two cups of coffee beside him. He stood when he saw me, reading my face.

"How'd it go?"

"It's done." I sank down beside him and took the coffee. "He's exactly who I thought he was. Maybe worse."

Cam didn't reach for me. He stared at the cooling coffee in his hands, his jaw set hard. "I keep seeing it," he said, voice low. "The way you stayed. Every day you went back to that house, knowing something was wrong, you were choosing a path that damn near led to your own funeral, shits crazy." I felt the sting of it, the raw, ugly honesty of his fear. "I was paralyzed, Cam. I didn't think I had anywhere to go."

"You had me," he said, finally looking at me, eyes bright with a frustration he'd been polite enough to hide until now. "But you didn't trust me. And I'm struggling to believe you won't just disappear into the shadows again the next time life gets heavy." The silence that followed wasn't comfortable, it was a jagged rough thing, stripped of the easy relief of the trial. We had to sit with the fact that survival wasn't the same thing as trust. But as he finally reached out to take my hand, his grip was firm, a tether rather than just comfort. "We have to be honest," I whispered. "Even when it's ugly." "Especially then," he agreed.

"I've been thinking," Cam said finally. "About us. About what comes next."

My heart quickened. "Yeah?"

He turned to face me, taking both my hands. "I know you need time. I know you're still figuring out who you are outside of everything that happened. And I respect that, Evie. I do." He paused, thumb tracing circles on my palm. "But I also know that I love you. Not the girl you were in high school, not the woman you thought you had to be for Sebastian. I love you, the person you're becoming. The one who dances in her living room and writes in journals and goes to therapy and does the hard work."

Tears filled the rim of my eyes. "Cam..."

"Nah, let me finish." He smiled, nervous now. "I don't want to rush you. But I also don't want to waste any more time pretending I don't know what I want." He reached into his pocket and pulled out a small velvet box. "So, I'm asking you now, even though the timing might not be perfect, even though we're both still healing, will you marry me?

Will you build a life with me, whatever that looks like?"

I looked at the ring—simple, elegant, nothing like the ostentatious diamond Sebastian had given me. Through the parlor window, I could see Grandma Locust watching us, hand pressed to her heart, beaming.

"Yes," I whispered. "Yes, I'll marry you."

Cam's face broke into the widest smile I'd ever seen. He slipped the ring onto my finger, and then he was kissing me and I was laughing and crying at the same time. Grandma Locust came rushing out and pulled us both into a fierce hug.

"About damn time," she said, wiping her own eyes. "I've been waiting for this since you two were sixteen years old."

- ✧ -

We didn't want to rush into getting married, but we also didn't want to waste any more time being apart. We thought we would take our time, building our relationship on honesty and patience but that wasn't how it went down. Cam moved into my garden apartment in the Brownstone I shared with Grandma Locust, and we learned each other's rhythms—how he liked his coffee, how I needed quiet in the mornings, how we both talked through movies and didn't mind.

Three months after the engagement, I woke up nauseous. I thought it was wedding nerves. But when the feeling persisted, I took a test.

Positive.

I stared at the two pink lines, heart racing. This wasn't planned. We'd talked about kids someday, but not yet, not while I was still in therapy, still figuring myself out. But as the initial shock faded, something else bloomed in my chest—joy. Pure, uncomplicated joy.

When I told Cam, he picked me up and spun me around, laughing. "We're having a baby," he kept saying, like he couldn't quite believe it.

"We're having a baby."

- ✧ -

The day of our wedding arrived warm and golden. I stood in Grandma Locust's bedroom, adjusting my simple white dress, one hand resting on my barely-there bump. Four months along, just starting to show if you knew where to look.

"You ready, baby girl?" Grandma asked, straightening my veil.

I looked at my reflection, I mean I really looked. The woman staring back wasn't the broken girl who'd left Sebastian, or the lost soul who'd started therapy. She was someone new.

"Yeah, Grams," I said. "I'm ready."

As I walked down the aisle toward Cam, surrounded by everyone I loved, something settled into place, a feeling of rightness I hadn't felt before. This was my life. Messy at times, imperfect, beautiful. And I was finally, truly living it.

When we exchanged vows, Cam's voice was steady and sure. "I promise to love you through the healing and the growing. Through the easy days and the hard ones. Through every version of yourself you become."

"I promise to let you," I replied, tears streaming down my face. "To let myself be loved. To build something real with you. To be brave enough to be happy."

As we kissed, sealing our promises, I felt the baby flutter, it was just the faintest movement, like a whisper of possibility. Our future, beginning right now.

The reception was everything I'd never known I wanted, intimate, joyful, full of laughter and dancing. When Cam and I took the floor for our first dance, he pulled me close, his hand resting on my stomach.

"Thank you," he whispered.

"For what?"

"For giving us a chance. For doing the work. For being brave enough to start over."

I looked up at him, this man who'd waited for me, who'd loved me through everything. "Thank you for waiting," I said. "For seeing me when I couldn't see myself."

As we swayed to the music, surrounded by love and light and hope, I knew this was just the beginning. There would be challenges ahead, parenthood, marriage, the ongoing work of healing. But for the first time in my life, I wasn't afraid.

I was ready. And I was enough.

Chapter 20

DOMINIQUE'S ROOM

The maple floor was warm and solid beneath my feet, built to catch you when you fell. I stood in the center of the studio, and for the first time, the air felt like my own. I wasn't an exhibit anymore. I was the architect.

Dominique's Room was more than a community center. It was a reclamation project. I'd spent months stripping the old wallpaper off this Bed-Stuy storefront, scraping away layers of grit and neglect until the brick beneath breathed again. I wanted a place where women from this neighborhood could bring their shadows and turn them into movement. A sanctuary where the weight of a mother's absence or a partner's cruelty could become something you danced through instead of drowned in. I wanted what I'd found for myself in that Greenpoint studio, but I wanted it here, where the roots were deep and the soil was familiar.

Justin and Bella had arrived early to help with the final touches. Justin was fussing over the placement of the "Dominique's Room" logo near the entrance—a minimalist, elegant script he'd designed himself, head tilted at the wall like he was critiquing someone's fashion choice. Bella was in the kitchenette, arranging platters of food with the same energy she brought to everything, insisting on colors that popped: hibiscus tea and citrus tarts, a deliberate contrast to the muted, grayscale life I'd nearly died in.

Justin had quit the firm three months ago—finally walked out the same day the VP gave the Goldman account to a junior analyst who'd done a third of the work. He'd sent me a voice memo at midnight: "I finally flipped that table, sis. Peacefully. With my head held high."

Now he ran his own boutique advisory practice out of a Harlem co-working space, with three clients deep and growing. He'd been the one to design the Dominique's Room logo pro bono, working on it between client calls, texting me font options at 2 a.m. like it was the most important project of his career. Maybe it was.

Kiki burst through the front door with the force of a summer storm, arms full of sunflowers, my nephew Ethan trailing behind her with a box of programs. She looked around the space, and her eyes landed on the memorial wall in the corner. There, among fresh gardenias, was a framed photograph of my mother. Not the woman lost to the fog of her own demons—this was Dominique just hitting twenty, laughing, her hair a wild halo, her eyes bright with a fire that addiction hadn't yet managed to dampen. Those unsent letters I'd found in Grandma Locust's steamer trunk had given me this version of her. They'd given me a woman who loved me through the static, and tonight, she was the guest of honor.

"Eve," Kiki whispered, her usual volume momentarily silenced. She walked over and squeezed my hand; her grip was warm and solid.

"She would have lived in this place. She would never have

left."

"That's the point, Kiki," I said, my voice steady despite the flutter in my chest. "Nobody has to leave their soul at the door here."

The room began to fill as the evening deepened. The neighborhood poured in—faces I'd known since childhood and new ones drawn by the promise of something honest. Grandma Locust arrived like royalty, draped in a deep purple shawl, her cane tapping a rhythmic cadence on the maple floor. She didn't say much at first. She walked the perimeter of the room, her hand trailing along the ballet barres as if she were blessing the wood. When she reached me, she leaned in, the scent of cinnamon clinging to her.

"You built a bridge, Eve," she said, her eyes milky but sharp. "Just make sure you're the one who decides who gets to cross it."

Camden was the last to arrive. He didn't make a scene—just appeared in the doorway, his broad shoulders filling the frame, a quiet anchor in the swirling energy of the party. He wore a simple black button-down, his cinnamon-brown skin glowing in the warm light. When our eyes met, the noise of the room fell away, leaving only the steady, resonant hum of what we'd built between us. Not the frantic, desperate hunger of our earlier stolen moments. Something durable.

Peace.

He walked over and didn't say a word, just placed his hand on my growing belly and then on the small of my back. The heat of his palm seeped through my silk dress, a silent affirmation. He knew what this night cost me. He knew about the nights I'd woken up gasping, the water of that bathtub still haunting my lungs, and he knew how many hours I'd spent in therapy with

Dr. Chen, unlearning the habit of making myself small.

When it was time for the dedication, I stepped onto the small, raised platform Justin had built. The crowd hushed—the rustle of silk and the clink of glasses fading into a heavy, expectant silence. I looked out at the faces. The people who had seen me break and the people who had helped me find the pieces. My hand drifted to my throat, not out of nervousness, but to feel my own pulse.

"My mother used to say that some people are born with too much rhythm for their own bodies," I began, my voice carrying into the corners of the room. "She spent her life trying to find a place to put that rhythm, a place where it wouldn't be judged or exploited or dimmed. She didn't find it. But she left me the map."

I looked at the photo of Dominique, then back at the women in the front row. "This room isn't just about dancing. It's about the right to occupy space. It's about the fact that your trauma is a part of your story, but it isn't the ending. We are more than the things that were done to us. We are the movement that comes after."

The applause was a warm wave, a collective exhale that made the mirrors tremble. For a few glorious hours, the world was exactly what I'd imagined it could be. I danced with Bella, laughed with Justin, held Grandma Locust as she watched the younger girls from the block tentatively try out the floor. I felt translucent and unbreakable—a woman who had finally stepped out of the shadow of a man's "care."

The unwelcome interruption happened at nine o'clock. It didn't come as a crash, nor a scream. It came as a man in a nondescript gray suit who stood by the entrance, looking entirely out of place among the vibrant colors and the soul music. He didn't join the celebration. He waited with a clinical patience that made the hair on my arms stand up—the kind of stillness I remembered from Sebastian's associates, men who moved through the world like they were auditing it.

I felt Cam stiffen beside me before I even reached the man. The music seemed to sour, the notes going metallic. I stepped away from the group, my heels clicking on the maple floor. The man didn't smile. He reached into his breast pocket and pulled out a thick white envelope.

"Eve Whitmore?" he asked, voice flat.

"Yes," I said, my heart already beating frantically.

"You've been served." He handed me the envelope and turned on his heel, gone as quickly as he'd entered. The cold draft he left behind felt like a weather front moving through the foyer.

I didn't open it immediately. I stood there, the white paper an intrusion against the maple and the brick. Kiki and Bella drifted toward me, their faces sharp with concern. Cam moved to my side, his shadow swallowing mine the way Sebastian's used to—except this felt like a shield, not a cage.

"Eve? What is it?" Kiki asked, her hand hovering near my shoulder.

I tore the envelope open. The legal header was familiar—the Whitmore's' preferred firm, a name that smelled of old money and power that doesn't accept defeat. A subpoena. An evidentiary hearing for an appeal. Sebastian's defense team was moving to overturn the conviction, and they weren't just attacking the evidence. They were coming after me.

"They're appealing," I whispered, the words tasting like copper.

"They're going after my past. They're going after us, Cam."

The room tilted, just a fraction. The ghost of that visual distortion from months ago flickered behind my eyelids. The Whitmore's were using their deep pockets to buy a second chance at my destruction. They wanted to dissect my time in Bed-Stuy, my relationship with my mother, every pill I'd taken to survive Sebastian's "love." They wanted to turn this center—this tribute to healing—into evidence of my supposed delusion.

Justin stepped closer, jaw tight. "They can't do that shit! The evidence was clear. The toxicology, the insurance policy, the forgery."

"They don't need a total victory, Justin," I said, looking at the subpoena like it was a venomous thing. "They just need to create enough noise to make me look like an unreliable witness. They want to drag me back into the dark so they can turn the lights off again."

I looked around my beautiful, vibrant room. The sunflowers Kiki brought were still bright, but the shadows in the corners seemed longer now. Having my private life, my pain, my recovery laid bare in another courtroom—it felt like a suffocating shroud. They wanted to make me prove I was worth living, all over again.

Cam took the papers from my hand. He went through them slowly, his face a mask of controlled intensity. When he finished, he didn't look defeated. He looked at me, and his eyes were flint hitting steel.

"Let them look, Eve," he said, voice low and steady. "Let them dig up every ghost they think they found. It doesn't change what happened in that bathroom. It doesn't change shit. You are who you are now."

"They'll try to say I used you," I said, a stray tear cutting through my makeup. "They'll try to say this was all a plan."

"They can say whatever they want in a courtroom," Cam replied, stepping into my space until our foreheads nearly touched. "But they don't live in this head. They don't live in this heart. You aren't that woman who needed to hide anymore. You're the woman who built all this here."

He gestured to the room, the mirrors and the barres and the photograph of my mother. "If they want a fight, we'll give them one. But we do it with the lights on. We do it with the truth. You don't have to carry this alone, Eve. Not ever again."

Grandma Locust had moved toward us, her presence a silent, formidable force. She looked at the papers in Cam's hand and then at me. She didn't offer platitudes. She simply reached out and adjusted the strap of my dress—a small, grounding gesture of care.

"A house built on truth can't be blown down by a lie, daughter," she said, her voice like old parchment. "It might shake. The windows might rattle. But the foundation stays."

I took a deep breath. I looked at the legal papers, then at the women still dancing in the studio, unaware of the storm brewing at the door. Sebastian hadn't just tried to kill me—he'd tried to own the ending of my story. This appeal was his final attempt to keep the book closed.

I wouldn't let him. I'd spent too long as a spectator in my own life, watching the movie of my trauma playing out while I sat silent in the dark. This room, Dominique's Room, was the first chapter I'd written for myself. The place where I'd learned that healing wasn't about the absence of the past—it was the ability to dance through the echoes it left behind.

I reached out and took the subpoena back from Cam. I didn't crumble it. I didn't hide it. I walked it over to the small desk in the corner and placed it next to the guest book—a reminder that staying free was never a finished project. The shadows of the past were still fighting for relevance. But they were just shadows. They only had the power I gave them.

"Justin," I called out, my voice finding its strength. "Turn the music up."

He looked at me—a question in his eyes—but when he saw the set of my jaw, he nodded. A moment later, a deep, percussive bass filled the room, a beat that demanded movement. I walked back into the center of the floor, feet finding their rhythm, body remembering its strength. The legal threat was a cloud. I was the sun, and I had no intention of setting.

I looked at my reflection in the mirror. Not a woman on the brink. A woman who had already fallen, hit the pavement, and decided to dance on it. The Whitmore's had their money and their secrets. I had the truth and I had the music, and for the first time, I knew that was enough. I wasn't just surviving the night anymore.

I owned it.

EPILOGUE

INHERITING THE FUTURE, FIVE MONTHS LATER

The contraction arrived like a freight train on a rusted track—a low-frequency vibration that started in my marrow and expanded until there was no room for air. I gripped the edge of the birth tub, knuckles white against the smooth recycled plastic. This was different water than the stagnant pool in Sebastian's master suite. That water had been a shroud, a chemically induced veil designed to pull me under. This water was warm and alive, scented with lavender and sweat. It didn't feel like drowning. It felt like it was a rising.

"Breathe through it, Eve. Just like we practiced. Ride the wave, don't let it crash over you," Cam whispered. His voice was a steady anchor in the storm, his hand a warm, calloused weight on my shoulder. He didn't look like a movie hero—he looked like a man who had seen the bottom of the world and decided to climb back up, one agonizing inch at a time. His cinnamon-brown skin slick with humidity, his eyes fixed on mine with a ferocity that was pure devotion, not possession.

I exhaled; it was a ragged, guttural sound that seemed to vibrate the foundations of the Brooklyn birth center. The room was bathed in the soft amber glow of salt lamps, a stark contrast to the fluorescent glare of the life I'd left behind. In the corner, Grandma Locust sat in a rocking chair, her presence a silent benediction. She didn't say much. She didn't have to. The rhythmic creak of the wood under her weight was the heartbeat of the room, a reminder that I came from a line of women who knew how to endure, how to turn pain into purpose.

The world narrowed to a single, white-hot point. The pain was no longer a guest—it was the master of the house. I felt my body stretching, tearing, reclaiming itself from years of being a museum exhibit for a man who only loved the frame. I thought of the bathtub in Jersey, the way I'd felt my consciousness flickering out like a dying bulb. I'd been so small then, a ghost in my own skin, waiting for permission to exist. Now I was a fucking mountain! I was the earth itself, shifting and cracking to make room for something new.

"She's almost here, Eve. I can see her," Cam murmured, voice thick with an emotion that made my own heart stutter. He wasn't looking at me with the clinical focus Sebastian had once used to measure my temperature. He was looking at me with awe, like I was the first wonder of the world.

I reached back, my hand finding Grandma Locust's. Her skin was like dark parchment, thin and translucent, but her grip was strong like iron. She leaned forward, breath smelling of peppermint and the ancient, earthy wisdom of the neighborhood. "Push, baby," she whispered. "Push through baby. Push this baby into the light. You ain't just bringing her in. You're bringing yourself back."

I screamed—a sound that wasn't about agony but about the absolute, terrifying power of creation. The sound of a cage door being ripped off its hinges. And then, with a final, searing surge of effort, the weight vanished. The room fell into a breathless silence, followed by a sharp, indignant wail that filled every corner of the space. The most beautiful sound I had ever heard—a high-frequency declaration of independence.

They placed her on my chest, a warm, slick weight that smelled of salt and the stars. She was perfect: tiny, squirming, a shock of dark hair and eyes already seeking the light. I looked down at her, my vision blurred by tears that were finally, for the first time in my life, not about grief. She was the inheritance I had worked for; the future Sebastian had tried to steal before it even had a name.

In the quiet of the birth center, the sun began to peek over the Brooklyn skyline, warming the maple floor, the wood solid and grounding beneath my feet. Cam was asleep in the chair next to the bed, head tilted back, finally at peace. Grandma Locust had gone home to rest, leaving me alone with the small, breathing weight in my arms.

I reached for my phone on the nightstand.

There was a notification from Mr. Vance, my attorney, that Sebastian's last appeal was denied. He was being moved to general population to serve out his sentence. Finished. I looked at the digital signature on the document: Eve Sterling. I'd taken the last name of the man of my dreams, severing the last thread he could ever hope to pull.

I opened the gallery. Thousands of photos. Sebastian at the gala, his lips brushing my brow like a dry leaf. Sebastian in the hallway, a clinical peck. Sebastian in the garden, a cold touch. Sebastian in the kitchen, the ghost of a kiss. Messages filled with his "care," his subtle negging, the "little blue pills" he'd used to decorate my cage. I looked at his face one last time and felt nothing. No anger. No fear. Just a profound, hollow boredom. He wasn't a villain in a noir film anymore.

He was just a man who had chosen power over peace and lost both.

I hit the select button. I scrolled through years of carefully curated lies, highlighting every image of his expensive life and cold marble floors. I selected the messages, the voicemails, the digital tethers that had kept me bound to a man who saw me as an exhibit. And then, with a thumb that didn't tremble, I hit delete.

"Are you sure you want to permanently delete these items?" the screen asked.

I looked down at the baby. She had drifted off to sleep, her tiny hand curled into a fist against my heart. I thought of the names we had chosen. Dominique, for the mother who had loved me through the fog of her own war. And Linda, for the grandmother who had held the line until I could find my way back. Dominique Linda Sterling. A bridge between the past we survived and the future we were building.

"Yes," I whispered to the empty room. "I'm sure."

The screen went blank for a second, digital purgatory—then returned to the home screen. The ghosts were gone. No more copper taste on my tongue, no more distortion in the road. The world didn't tilt to the right anymore. It was level, open, drenched in morning light.

I leaned my head back against the pillow, listening to the soft, rhythmic puff of my daughter's breath. I had spent my life waiting for men to tell me who I was, only to find that the answer was written in the very blood and bone they tried to break. I wasn't a detour. I wasn't a victim. I was the architect of the air I breathed. I had spent so long running from myself, I didn't realize peace was waiting for me to stand still... and when I did, I was no longer restless.

www.ingramcontent.com/pod-product-compliance
Lightning Source LLC
LaVergne TN
LVHW090942080826
845145LV00003B/849

* 9 7 8 0 9 7 8 9 5 9 9 3 7 *